Henry M. Field

Blood is Thicker Than Water

A Few Days Among our Southern Brethren

Henry M. Field

Blood is Thicker Than Water
A Few Days Among our Southern Brethren

ISBN/EAN: 9783337142490

Printed in Europe, USA, Canada, Australia, Japan

Cover: Foto ©Andreas Hilbeck / pixelio.de

More available books at **www.hansebooks.com**

BLOOD IS THICKER THAN WATER:

A FEW DAYS AMONG

OUR SOUTHERN BRETHREN.

BY HENRY M. FIELD, D.D.

AUTHOR OF "FROM THE LAKES OF KILLARNEY TO THE GOLDEN HORN,"
"FROM EGYPT TO JAPAN," "ON THE DESERT," "AMONG THE HOLY HILLS,"
AND "THE GREEK ISLANDS AND TURKEY AFTER THE WAR."

NEW YORK
GEORGE MUNRO, PUBLISHER
1886

CONTENTS.

vi CONTENTS.

PREFACE.

THE author of this little volume disclaims any responsibility for its appearance. The several chapters were written as letters to the paper in New York of which he is editor, and as such served the purpose for which they were intended. Nor did he wish to give any further importance to such slight sketches. They were too personal: and whatever of interest they might have to members of the party as a souvenir of a pleasant excursion, or to friends here and there who had welcomed it in their hospitable homes, they were of no importance to the general public. And yet for some cause they had met with a reception which was wholly unexpected. Northern readers were gratified by the pictures of that New South which was taking the place of the Old; of its new life, new industries, and new ambitions; while a deeper impression was made in the South itself. Nobody could have been more surprised than the writer at the way they were copied in Southern papers, and spoken of in terms which seemed to him altogether extravagant. Seeing this, friends have

asked permission to have them reprinted, believing that
in this form they might be circulated more widely, and do
still further good. This is a consideration quite apart
from that of literary merit, and it is this which has per-
suaded him to yield to a wish so kindly expressed. If what
has thus come into existence " without premeditation "
shall serve to promote a better feeling between the North
and the South, its purpose will be fully answered.

BLOOD IS THICKER THAN WATER.

I.

THROUGH VIRGINIA AND THE CAROLINAS—KING'S MOUNTAIN—OVER THE BORDER INTO GEORGIA.

WHEN Mr. Andrew Carnegie wrote his book, "An American Four-in-Hand in Britain," it took the public by its very title. There was something captivating in the idea of seeing the Old Country once more in the good, old-fashioned way, from the top of a coach, with the horses going at full speed, and the guard blowing his horn; now mounting over the breezy downs, and now trotting swiftly along the quiet lanes, between the hedge-rows; reining up here and there in some quaint village, or turning aside to visit some ancient castle or cathedral; and thus, in the magnificent drive of a few days, seeing so much of the beauty and the glory of England. To such a journey no contrast could be greater than one by rail, which is, of all modes of travel, the most prosaic and commonplace; which is indeed so dull and dreary as only to be thought of with satisfaction when it is over. But there are compensations in all things. The latter mode of locomotion is swifter, and enables one to traverse a wider space; to sweep over more degrees of latitude and longitude; and thus to

see more lands and people. Especially if a party sets out
in a private car, and with an engine all to itself, it is master of time and space, and able to move at will, travelling
by night, and appearing with each morning in some new
city or State. Nor is it only as an economy of time that
a flying trip has its advantages: it has its pleasures
also, as I hope to show to those who will keep me company
in a rapid journey in the South.

It was near the end of Winter, which had been long and
cold. After months of ice and snow, the air was still
sharp and keen, and while shivering in the chilling winds,
one could not but feel a desire to flee away, at least for a
brief respite, to a milder clime, and just then came the
opportunity. It came in this way: though I am a dweller in
a great city, where I have passed a busy life for thirty-one
years, I have a home in the country, among the Berk-
shire Hills where I was born, to which I fly at the approach
of Summer. Thither came last year a gentleman whom I
had never seen before. He was a Southerner, who, though
in the prime of manhood (a little turned of forty), was old
enough to have been in the war. He had been a Confederate soldier, who surrendered with Johnston, and then came
North, with his parole in one pocket, and less than a hundred dollars in the other; and here, with nothing to depend
upon but his own clear head and honest heart, began what
proved an extraordinary career. Though he seldom spoke
of business, I learned from others that he was a cotton
merchant of New York, who in a few years had risen to
the top, and was sometimes styled the cotton king. He
was a native of East Tennessee, and it was perhaps because
it recalled the scenery of that mountain region, that he
took such a fondness for our Hill Country. Every day he
was driving about, enjoying the endless succession of hill
and valley, wood and stream. From being near neighbors,
we soon became friends; and hence it was that I received a

letter from this gentleman, Mr. John H., Inman, saying that he was about to make a trip South with several friends, and inviting me to be of the party.

It was at four o'clock in the afternoon of a day in February, in this year of grace 1886, that we went on board the private car of the President of the Louisville and Nashville Railroad, which had been placed at our service, as two of our company were Directors. Except a son of Rev. Dr. John Hall, who had received the same invitation as myself, I did not know one of the guests, and looked with a curious eye into the faces of those who were to be our companions for a couple of weeks. They were all representative men. Mr. Cornelius N. Bliss is a well-known merchant of New York. Mr. J. A. Bostwick was one of the founders of the Standard Oil Company, which is ready to light the world; as Mr. H. O. Armour, of the great Chicago house, is ready to feed it; and Mr. Inman and Mr. Bliss, representing the Southern cotton, to clothe it; and Mr. Thomas Rutter, and Mr. Charles H. Bosher, both well-known railroad men, to cast up highways for the nation to pass over. Thus we had, with our host himself, a round half dozen "capitalists," making a rather formidable company. But whatever they might be in Wall street, whether "bulls" or "bears" or ravening wolves, in our little circle they were very quiet gentlemen, each disposed to contribute to the happiness of all. Mr. Inman took one of his clerks along to see to our letters and telegrams and baggage, so that we had not to look after anything.

But the description of our party would not be complete without mention of its general factotum. "Robert" is a native of Jamaica, who in his early days took to the sea, and went on voyages to Liverpool. Then he sailed from Boston in a ship laden with ice for Calcutta, and spent several years in the East Indies, of which I had many talks

with him, and found him very intelligent. Now he is a
retainer of the Nashville and Louisville Company, and the
conductor of its President's car. He was the general pro-
vider for our table, though there was a cook besides, and
cared for us so well that not once (except in the cities,
where we spent a day or two) did we go to a hotel. In all
things necessary for our comfort, he watched over us like
an uncle, and to his faithfulness we owe much of the pleasure of our journey. Thus freed from care, with nothing to
do but to enjoy ourselves, we took our seats in a sort of
family group, and whirled away.

I am an old traveller, and yet there is always a little
sinking of the heart when I go from home, not knowing
what changes may take place during the time of separation.
But the swift motion acts upon me like a breeze at sea,
blowing away sad thoughts, and turning me from that
which is left behind to that which is before.

Our special car was constructed for sight-seeing, a room
at the end being fitted up with plate-glass on every side;
and as this car was placed at the end of the train, one had
but to sit here to have an unobstructed view of the country
over which we passed. My favorite place was in an easy-
chair close to the end, looking out upon the landscape from
which we were fleeing away at the rate of forty miles an
hour. If I had been caught up in the chariot of Elijah, I
could hardly have had more of the sense of being carried
through the air. And

"Now fades the glimmering landscape on the sight."

Watching the lights in the villages as we went rushing by,
I made to myself pictures of the people that lived in them—
the family gathering at the close of day, the father coming
home from his store or shop, the dear mother at the table,
and the boys and girls seated round the shaded lamp or

the open fire. What a joy to think that our country has millions of such happy homes!

As we passed through Baltimore, or rather under it, by a tunnel a mile and a half long, a remark from one of the company informed me that this was the work of our fellow-traveller, Mr. Rutter, who is known throughout the country as the Great Tunneller, having made a specialty of this branch of engineering, which has wrought such miracles in Europe, in boring under the Alps, through the Mont Cenis and the St. Gothard.

It was eleven o'clock when we reached Washington; but as I walked down the platform, I recognized the form of a certain Judge, whose brotherly greeting always makes my heart beat quicker, though we had but a few minutes together, when our train steamed out of the station, and bore away into the night.

And now appeared the extreme courtesy of my *compagnons de voyage.* On this car was a room reserved for the President, which contained a double bed, a writing-table and three windows. This they proposed to give up to me. I felt a great delicacy in accepting it, but they insisted, and so I had "the king's chamber" for my sole use and occupancy; while the half dozen capitalists, representing (according to the veracious accounts of the reporters of Southern papers) not less than fifty millions, "bunked" together in upper and lower berths, like common mortals! The deference of the "lords temporal" to the one "lord spiritual" was never more fully illustrated.

It was midnight when we crossed the Potomac at Alexandria, which but a few years since was girdled with forts bristling with guns. Whether the forts are now dismantled, I know not; but if the guns are still there, they are silent; not a sound of war breaks the Sabbath-like stillness of the place, as we bear away from the river, and soon cross the field of Manassas, twice stained with fraternal blood. This part of Virginia was "the dark and bloody ground" of the War. Our route by the Virginia Midland Railroad leads us across the State. From the time of leaving the Potomac, we ascend slowly but perceptibly, till (although we do not at any point cross the Blue Ridge) we are among its foot-hills. The Piedmont Air Line (a part of the Richmond and Danville system), which stretches from Washington City to Atlanta, takes its name from the fact that it runs on the hills, rather than in the valleys. Lynchburg, on the upper waters of the James River, is the retreat to which Gen. Lee sought to escape with his army after the fall of Richmond, and where he hoped, with the natural defences of the mountains, to be able to make a further stand and prolong the struggle. Appomattox, at which, overtaken and surrounded by Grant and Sheridan, he was compelled to surrender, is but a few miles distant.

At Danville we had another proof that we were getting South in *a change of gauge*, that of the Southern railway system being five feet, while that of the North is but four feet eight and a half inches. This seemed to us rather a formidable matter, but it was done with a facility that surprised us. The train was run into a frame-work of heavy timbers, where our huge Pullman car was lifted into air by screws worked by hydraulic machinery, and the wheels with the whole supporting gear run out, and that with the broader gauge run in, and the car was settled into its place. The change hardly took five minutes. But with long trains it must be a serious delay; and we are glad to know that it is soon to be done away with. In a few weeks the gauge of the whole railway system of the South is to be changed to conform to that of the North. It will cost millions, but the object is thought to be worth it all. May we not interpret this as a happy symbol of other changes by which the course of things North and South is hereafter to be run on the same track to the end of a common prosperity?

At day-break we were in the heart of Old Virginia, and at noon stopped at Charlotte in North Carolina. While the other passengers on the train were taking their dinner, we (having ours in our own car) were at leisure to take a sun-bath in the warmth that we were now feeling for the first time. It was delightful to be able to walk about without being muffled up in heavy overcoats. The air was so soft and balmy that we felt as if indeed the Winter was over and gone, and the time of the singing of birds had come.

As a Southern man, Mr. Inman might be expected to feel an interest in any prosperous Southern town, but to this was added a special interest here. Something in his eye seemed to say that he had seen the place before. It was only about six miles away that he took part in the great surrender of April, 1865, and received his parole as a prisoner of war! What changes time brings! Little thought the boy of that day—but twenty years old—that in twenty-one years more he would come back to that spot, not as a paroled soldier, but as a Northern merchant, and a prince among his brethren in the new home where it has been his lot to live, and (I may add) to achieve a success which could never have been his, had the fortune of war been other than it was. So does the great Ruler of events plan for us better than we know.

The station was alive with " colored folks " of both sexes and of every age, who would be a study to an artist, and furnish rich subjects for the pencil of Nast. One thing I observed with satisfaction—the absence of a cowed look, which is the badge of servitude stamped on the forehead. Now they are free, and show it in every motion. Look at that young buck mounted on a mule! His garments can hardly hold together, and yet he bestrides the beast as proudly as if he were Alexander the Great. There is a dash of independence in every kick of his long legs, and the rags that wave from his tattered coat seem as if conscious that they float in the air of freedom.

There was one group that were evidently prepared for a migration. On inquiry, we learned that they were bound for Kansas! It seemed a strange venture for these poor creatures—old " mammies," with their sons and daughters and little grandchildren—to wander so far away from the place where they were born. But may not the Guiding Hand still lead them on? Mr. Armour tells me that, in their great yards and packing-houses at Kansas City, some of their best employés are colored men. And who knows but these little pickaninnies, that now cling to their mothers' garments, may yet be the free and independent toilers of the mighty West?

For those who stay in the old North State, Charlotte has an excellent training-school in Biddle University, whose fine building we saw as we entered the town. This is one of the most admirable institutions in the South for the higher education of the most promising young men of the colored race.

At Charlotte a gentleman of the country, who was known to some of the party, met us, and accompanied us a few miles on our way. As he was the owner of a cotton factory, and a large employer of labor, I asked: " How do you get along with the negroes now that they are free?" " Very well," he said, " although they are not suited to factory work so well as to the field. A negro works with his hands rather than his brain: he is a good field-hand—good at the hoe or the plow. But set him to watch a loom, where he has nothing to do but to keep his eyes wide open, and before he knows it those eyes will be shut and he be fast asleep. His place is in driving teams, cutting wood or drawing logs, or any kind of out-door labor." In this they are willing to work and for very moderate wages; although, as they have been bred in habits of improvidence (for as

long as they were slaves, they had no motive to save anything, it being the duty of their masters to take care of
them), they are apt to spend their money as fast as they
earn it. Their natural indolence often leads them, after
working a few days and getting a little ahead, to " lie off "
till it is spent, and then go to work again. For this reason
they are not always to be depended upon. To cure them
of this slipshod way of life is of course a work of time.
They must be educated to something better, and no doubt
will be, as they are a simple and docile race, although it
may take a whole generation to form them to habits of
economy and thrift and regular industry.

" And what has been the effect upon the whites of this
change of relation in the two races?" He said it had been
disastrous to the great land-owners, who were suddenly
stripped of the labor needed to cultivate their large plantations. But, on the other hand, where the change had
ruined one man, it had given ten a chance to rise. Before
the war there was no middle class between the slave-owners
and the " poor white trash." The rich planters owned all
the land, and all the labor to cultivate it. A man who
did not have slaves could only hoe the small patch of corn
around his little cabin in the woods, eking out his subsist-
ence by what he could get with his gun and his fishing-rod.
Now the old plantations are being broken up, and even a
poor man may earn enough by a year's labor to buy a few
acres; and though he could not buy a slave, he may be able
to *hire* one or two negroes to work for him; and if he be
himself capable and industrious, he will in a few years be
the owner of a small farm, and have the feeling of independence which belongs to a landed proprietor. Of course
all this involves a social change, somewhat like the breaking up of the Feudal System in France, when the great
estates of the nobles were divided, and passed into the hands
of their former peasantry. Such changes are always at-

tended with suffering to the aristocratic families, but in
the end they are for the greatest good of the greatest number.   The New South will come when the Carolinas, like
Massachusetts and Connecticut, instead of being the ter-
ritorial appanage of a few families, are divided up into tens
of thousands of small farms, cultivated by intelligent, independent, and self-respecting husbandmen.

While engaged in this conversation, we were running
along at a fearful rate.   The position of our car at the end
of the train, while it gave us advantages for sight-seeing,
had the disadvantage of being subject to the greatest motion, and it rocked from side to side like a ship at sea.
The engineer seemed to be on his mettle to show us what
he could do.   The engine hissed and snorted, and rushed
on like a wild horse of the desert, its guider " touching it
up" as a California driver would touch up a team of a
dozen mules with his mighty lash.   The road is full of
curves, and as we went round them at terrific speed, it
seemed as if our " driver " was cracking his whip with
such vigor that he might crack the tail off, and, as our car
was " the tail," he might leave us far behind.

Had we been in search of the grand or the picturesque,
we might have found it at several points by diverging a
little from our course.   A gentleman of New Orleans, who
has been a great traveller both in his own and in other
countries, speaks with enthusiasm of the mountain scenery
in the western part of North Carolina, where one lofty
peak, called Cæsar's Head, commands a view which he has
rarely seen equalled, although he is familiar not only with
all the mountain scenery of our own country, but with the
far loftier ranges of Mexico and Peru.   Without, however,
comparing it with the Cordilleras or the Andes, he thinks
it far surpasses the views of which we are wont to boast,
such as those in the White Hills, or any other in the United
States east of the Rocky Mountains.

As the day wears on, we come in sight of two spots of interest connected with the War of the Revolution. At a distance on the left rises King's Mountain, on the top of which was fought the battle of that name in 1780. Though the numbers were small as compared with battles of a later day, the engagement was one of the hardest-fought of the war, and was notable as one in which a body of militia gained a decisive victory over regular troops. Its results, too, gave it an importance at the South, like that of the Battle of Bennington at the North, as a turning-point in the war, since it gave a check to the army of Cornwallis, as Bennington gave to that of Burgoyne, and thus disarranged the whole British campaign. The plan had been for the English army, which landed in Charleston, to make that a base for operations against the Southern colonies. Having overrun South Carolina, it was to move North into Virginia, and take it by a fire in the rear, executing a movement not unlike that of Sherman in his march through Georgia. While Cornwallis marched North, Sir Henry Clinton, leaving New York, was to march South, and the two armies were to meet in Virginia, there to receive the final surrender of the great Rebellion. This finely planned campaign was entirely upset by the battle of King's Mountain, by which the advance of Cornwallis was delayed till the following spring; and when at last he reached Yorktown he had to defend himself against Washington, and not Washington only, but against a French army landed from the French fleet, which had just entered Chesapeake Bay. The combined armies caused the siege of Yorktown to end in a surrender quite other than that which had been planned by the British commanders. All this turn of war hung on the stubbornness with which those yeomen of the South (who had crossed the mountains from Eastern Tennessee) fought on that autumn day (it was the 7th of October). Their victory was complete. The English were defeated, and their

commander, Col. Ferguson, killed, and buried on the spot
where he fell.   The site of the battle is marked by a
monument on the crest of the mountain, which we can just
see as it catches the light of the setting sun.

A few miles further, we pass the famous field of Cowpens,
where that brave soldier, General Morgan, defeated the dashing cavalry officer, Colonel Tarleton.   Of this battle I used
to hear in my boyhood from an old negro who had been in
it, and who depicted in his simple way, and yet with no little
vividness, scenes that were still fresh in his memory.   How
far away all these events seem now, although they took place
but little more than a hundred years ago!   So completely
have the animosities of those days died out, that the places
of these battles are preserved simply as a matter of historic
interest.   So may it be with the battles of a more recent
war, that the hatreds and the bitterness shall pass away,
while the result achieved in the preservation of " union and
liberty " shall remain as a precious inheritance forever!

It was midnight when we rolled into the station at
Atlanta.   The city seemed to be asleep, but we soon found
that a portion of it at least was wide awake: for as we entered the Kimball House, we were dazzled with a blaze of
light, and heard a sound of festivity.   A Jewish festival
had gathered the Israelites from far and near—men and
women, young men and maidens—who had come together
to do it honor.   The seven-branched golden candlestick on
the windows told how they clung to every symbol of their
faith.   The great number of the Hebrew race in the cities
of the South, as of the North and West, is a very noticeable
fact.   But we were too weary to be kept awake by the sound
of music and mirth, and, after being jolted for thirty-two
hours, were glad to stretch ourselves in beds that would not
rock under us, and sleep the sleep of quietness and peace.

II.

ATLANTA is a new city, yet it is one of the historic places
of America. The war destroyed it, and the war has made it.
During the earlier campaigns, while Virginia was swept and
made desolate, Georgia suffered little. Its turn did not
come till the last year when it was to learn how terrible war is.
It is less than twenty-two years since General Sherman,
who had been steadily advancing, fighting at every step,
reached this city, and planted his batteries against it. This
brought the crisis of the war. Gen. Joseph E. Johnston was
removed, and General Hood placed in command, a change
which was immediately followed by a fierce attack on the
Union lines, which ended in a bloody repulse; and from this
point Sherman began his memorable march to the sea.

Naturally these are bitter memories for the South; and
yet such are the compensations which sometimes come
from war, that Atlanta, which was then destroyed, has so
fully recovered that it is now the most prosperous city in
the South. It has become a great railroad center, from
which lines radiate to all parts of the country. Hence it
draws to itself the trade and commerce, not only of
Georgia, but of surrounding States. The result is a business activity which one sees nowhere else.

The first sign of civilization to the eye of a traveller is a
good hotel. Judged by this standard, Atlanta stands in
the front rank of cities, at least in this portion of the country, as it has the best hotel we have seen in the Gulf States,
not excepting the St. Charles in New Orleans. When we

were here two years ago, the old Kimball House had been burned to the ground. But out of its ashes it has risen again, far grander than before, of fine architectural proportions, with wide halls and lofty ceilings; rooms ample in size and handsomely furnished; and all the "modern improvements" of the best hotels at the North. I am not surprised to learn that commercial travellers, who make their business tours through the South, try to come round to Atlanta for Sunday, to wash off the dust of the week in warm baths; to sleep in clean, sweet beds, and get a "square meal;" and thus refresh themselves for the campaign of the week that is to follow.

The rebuilding of the Kimball House is a fair type of the rebuilding of Atlanta itself. Never was there a more complete recovery from ruin. Twenty-two years ago this valley among the hills was like the Valley of Gehenna, into which shot and shell were poured, as fire from heaven fell upon Sodom and Gomorrah. Besieged, bombarded, and burned, it seemed as if its fate was to be swept from the face of the earth. Yet the besom of destruction that swept away the old city but cleared a wider space for the new. Instead of the land being sown with salt, that it might not bear any green thing, on this very spot, blasted by fire, has sprung up the representative city of that New South which is to take the place of the Old. Atlanta is the first-born Child of the Resurrection, and has rightfully taken the place of the first-born, as the Capital of this Empire State of the South.

Of the rapid growth of Atlanta, we had full proof this morning as some friends called with carriages to take us about. There was nothing of the sleepy, half-dead look of a Southern city in the old days. The streets were full of busy life. Shops and stores and banks were open, with the same look of activity and prosperity that may be seen in the most enterprising Northern city. Buildings were going up in every quarter. On all sides was heard the sound of the hammer, or of the stone-cutter, or the buzzing of the saw-mill, which was turning out the boards and timbers which were to enter into new dwellings and new warehouses. As Atlanta is in the heart of the Cotton Belt, and the growing of cotton is the chief business of the surrounding country, a Northern visitor is very much interested in the huge warehouses in which is stored the product of this great national industry. Take them all together, these warehouses must cover many acres, in which is piled up the growth of whole counties, and indeed of a large portion of the State.

Until recently the great difficulty in the handling of cotton in large quantities has been from its bulkiness. The precious commodity, being of a springy texture, bulged out in most unwieldy fashion. This difficulty is now removed by a gigantic "Compress," in which a weight of many tons is brought to bear upon a bale of cotton, squeezing it into one third its former space. It was very interesting to watch the operations of this monster, a huge Leviathan, which snapped up a bale of cotton as a whale might snap up a porpoise, crushing it with one grip of its tremendous jaws. Thus "flattened out," the bale is instantly held fast by bands of sheet-iron that are clamped around it. This compression of bulk is of immense importance in shipments of cotton abroad. A ship thus laden will not only carry three times as much, but its cargo is three times as safe against fire, that sometimes breaks out in a ship's hold, and, finding in the loose cotton an inflammable material, not unfrequently destroys both cotton and ship together.

After seeing the cotton in bulk, we paid a visit to some of the large sales-rooms, where hundreds of "samples" are spread out on long tables, and are examined with the greatest care, that the most delicate fibres may be selected for the finest products of the loom.

But while we looked with wonder at these evidences of material wealth, some of us were still more interested in the Public Schools, which Mr. Robert J. Lowry, the Chairman of the Board of Education, kindly volunteered to show us. These schools are a matter of city pride, and show how Atlanta is becoming like a Northern city, and Georgia like a Northern State, in this great matter of education. As we rode up to a large building on the top of a hill, we were startled by a cry of fire, at which a thousand children came pouring out of the different doors. They seemed to move with remarkable composure, and we soon learned that this was merely an exercise of discipline, to accustom the pupils to self-control; so that, in case of a real danger, they might not fall into a panic, which is often a cause of greater loss than the fire itself. When the exercise was over, and the pupils had had a sniff of the fresh morning air, they returned to the uninjured building, where Mr. Grady, of "The Atlanta Constitution," who is the general favorite in this city, made some very happy remarks, which put everybody in the best of humor. Thus we made the round of several schools, which gave me the same sort of pleasure which I find in visits to the schools of my native New England.

But somehow or other (I can not tell exactly how it was) it was the Atlanta University, for colored young men and women, which gave me a deeper feeling than mere satisfaction. The pupils were not mere children, but young men and women. We had no time for recitations, but they sung to us in such a way that, before I knew it, I was trying to choke something in my throat. It seems as if God had bestowed upon this race the gift of song to lighten their humble and lowly lot. In the days of servitude, they sung on the old plantations songs that have still a strange power. It will show how well acquainted I am with Southern geography, that one of my first questions was " Where is the

Suwanee river?" so often had I found myself humming, even when on the other side of the globe:

> " 'Way down on the Suwanee River
>
> . . . .
>
> There's where the old folks stay,"

a song that never has such a flavor of home as when sung by rich African voices. And when it comes to religion, it seems as if the loneliness and sorrow of years were poured forth in the wailing cry:

> " Nobody knows the sorrows I've seen—
> Nobody knows but Jesus."

Sad hearts sing the sweetest songs, as crushed flowers yield the sweetest perfume, and it may be one purpose of God in permitting the African race such a long night of sorrow, that they might sing in pathetic strains the song of deliverance.

Next to general Education as an influence in raising the standard of public intelligence and public morality, is the victory recently gained in the cause of Temperance. Atlanta, as is well known, has lately been the scene of a fierce struggle; and although the storm is over, there is a long ground-swell, which shows how violently the sea of public opinion has been agitated. In the division into two strong parties, the greater portion of the Christian population have taken the Temperance side. To understand the attitude of the question in Georgia, it should be remembered that several years since the State passed a Local Option Law, which gave to each county (not city or township) the right to decide for itself whether it would permit the sale of intoxicating liquors. There was a special reason for some decided action. In every county there is a central point—it may be only a cross-roads, or it may be dignified as the site of the county court-house—which would be chosen by worthless fellows as the place to open the lowest "groggeries," which would soon make it the center of demoralization to the negroes in all the country round. In the old slavery days they could be kept on the plantations, and be subject to some sort of discipline, by which they could be guarded from temptation. But since they are their own masters, they can go to a "saloon" as freely as white folks, and stagger home with "the glorious sense of independence" of so many white drunkards. As they are fond of drink, they are tempted to steal cotton from their employers, that they may exchange it for bottles of whiskey. By this underground traffic, the planters are doubly injured —in being robbed of their cotton, and in the drunkenness of the class on which they are obliged to depend for labor. It is therefore a matter of self-protection to shut up these grog-shops: their own safety depends upon it. Nor do they have to wait for years to get a Prohibition law through the Legislature. With the right of Local Option, *they can enact a law for themselves*—a law which may be more effective than a general law, inasmuch as it is *their own act;* and having voted for it, they are personally interested to enforce it: they are at once the legislators and the executive.

In the cities, of course, the struggle was greater, and it has been particularly fierce here in Atlanta. There are large moneyed interests involved in the sale of whiskey, and these are supported by the mighty army of tipplers, big and little—the old topers and the petty swiggers—all banded together to maintain the freedom (!) to get drunk, and to sell that which makes men drunk.

Against this combination there was a body of earnest men and women, who had the welfare of the city at heart; and the community just then was keyed up to a high pitch of religious excitement by a revival which was in progress. Atlanta is the home of Sam Jones, the noted revivalist, who, with the ardor of a soldier, pitched into the fight, and, like a military leader, animated his followers, whom he inspired with a determination not to be seduced on the one hand, nor to be cowed on the other. Thus marshalled in ranks, they stood shoulder to shoulder, like one of Stonewall Jackson's old brigades, and fought the good fight to the bitter end.

But with all this they could not have won the battle without the help of the colored vote. For this both sides angled dexterously. But to the honor of the blacks be it said, they for the most part threw their votes on the side of Temperance. Many influences, social as well as political, contributed to this. As a race, they are fond of marching and music, and any cause which puts them in the ranks, and sets them to a kind of military drill, gives them an importance in their own eyes. Nor were they above the attentions of ladies of high social position, who opened booths. at which they gave to their dark-skinned allies "the cup that cheers but not inebriates"—an attention which was very flattering to Cæsar and Pompey. A glass of whiskey from the keeper of a grog-shop to an emancipated slave, was not half so sweet as a cup of tea or coffee from the hand of the daughter of his old master. By such means these fair advocates of Temperance won the hearts of the colored voters, with whom the streets were alive, as they paraded up and down, like soldiers marching to battle.

The day came, and the issue was doubtful. The battle was long and hard. But the end was a victory for the Temperance cause such as it has never had before.

But its enemies never give up. Defeated at the polls, they tried it in the courts. All sorts of legal quibbles were used to defeat the will of the people. Still so far their action has been sustained: and a lawyer engaged for the other side frankly admitted to me that he had little hope of reversing in the courts the decision which had been made at the polls.

Our colored brethren sometimes mix religion and politics in rather a strange way. Simple-hearted creatures as they are, they are apt to think that everybody who is on *their* side is on the Lord's side, and do not hesitate to ask the Lord to " be wery partic'lar," and " to see to it Hisself " that their friends are duly provided for. Governor Colquitt is said to have owed his great popularity to his entire freedom from pride: his readiness to stop in the most public place and talk with any poor man, asking after his welfare in a tone of real interest that made him feel that he was somebody, and did him " a heap o' good." This may account for such appeals as the following, with which a black Boanerges stormed the court of heaven. It was in a large meeting, when all were in a state of excitement, and their fervent " sighings " and " breathings " were audible over the house. In the midst of such a seething mass knelt a son of thunder, who, lifting up his voice to the mighty God of Jacob, exclaimed: " O Lord! we thank Thee that we have a Governor who is not ashamed to speak to the colored man when he meets him in the street, and to treat him like a brother! And if he should desire to be re-elected to the high office which he now holds, *we pray that he may be elected by a handsome majority!*" This certainly was " prevailing prayer," if not with the Lord, at least with the voters, who answered the petition with a chorus of fervent amens. A man who could rally such forces, earthly and heavenly, to his support, could hardly fail of his election.

I have spoken of Sam Jones, the revivalist, of whom I had heard nothing but his eccentricities. From certain expressions quoted in the papers, I had supposed him to be merely a mountebank. But I am told by those who know him well that he is a man of truly devout spirit, who is not at all anxious to make himself conspicuous, but is " in dead earnest " to save his fellow-men. Some intimate that he " lets off " these strange expressions to pique the curiosity of the multitude, believing that many who

"Come to scoff will remain to pray."

Mr. Grady, who has a knowledge of men that is quite sufficient to enable him to detect a charlatan, speaks of him as his friend, and as a man of genuine power, of honest convictions, and of a warm Christian heart. His illustrations, it must be confessed, are often homespun, and yet they are sometimes very apt. For example: " I was riding with him one day," said my informant, " when the conversation turned on the subject of Faith. I wanted a reason for everything, and could not understand how I must ' believe ' in order to be saved. ' I'll tell you how it is,' he said. ' Here's a farmer who has got a spring running into his barn-yard to water his cattle. He has fitted it up so that the pressure of a hoof on a plank, as a creature walks up to the trough, opens a pipe and sets the water running, and when the creature steps back, it closes, and the water in the trough runs off, to be filled again by the next comer. But now comes along a conceited young steer, that thinks this contrivance is all a humbug, and walks round the trough, and looks into it on the other side and sees it empty. and goes off in a huff, and lies down in a corner of the yard, and there lies day after day till it dies of thirst. It dies for the want of faith. It's just so in religion. Don't stop to reason about it, but walk right up to the spring, and drink and live.' ' "

Such conversations gave an added charm to our drives about Atlanta. Our sight-seeing ended in that which is the most pleasant of all sights, the interior of a Christian home, in which we were entertained at luncheon, where I was gratified to see that, with every variety and luxury on the table, not a drop of wine was set before the guests—an adherence to principle which was repeated a day or two after in one of the first residences of Nashville.

Again taking to our carriages we drove out the long avenues, which are lined with beautiful residences, the best proof of the general prosperity of this Southern capital.

The evening was reserved for a more general demonstration of good feeling, in a dinner given at the Kimball House, at which were present the Governor of the State, and the Mayor and leading residents of the city. For such hospitality I was quite unprepared, as were other members of the party, no one of us presuming to appropriate it to himself. We all knew that it was a mark of respect intended for our host, in which we were included as his guests. Wherever we come we find a general regard for Mr. Inman, which we are at no loss to understand. He is a son of the South, who shared her fortunes in her dark days, and who, coming North after the war, has had a success of which the people of his native State are proud, while they are still more gratified to see that he has never lost his affection for the land of his birth, and that his highest ambition is to do what he can to re-create its industry and restore its prosperity. Wherever he was called out, as he was at every place at which we stopped, though he spoke with great modesty, his few words needed no other eloquence than the spirit which they breathed. They were to the effect that, though he had lived for the last twenty years at the North, his heart was still here; and that if he had obtained any position of means or influence, whatever of ability or of experience or of credit he might possess which could be of benefit to the South, it was at her service—words which were uttered with such simplicity and genuine feeling that they produced a deep impression on every listener.

At the dinner Mr. Grady presided, enlivening the conversation with his wit and humor, and introducing the several speakers with a charm all his own. Naturally the first sentiment in Southern hearts was " Georgia," for she was "their mother," with which was coupled the name of her honored Executive. To this Governor McDaniel replied with great kindness, welcoming us, and all Northern men who would see for themselves the real condition of the South, to Georgia and her sister States, wishing that the Union now restored might never be broken.

Mr. Grady had referred to the war without reserve and without bitterness. Indeed he had paid a handsome tribute to General Sherman, though he said "he was not a very 'keerful' man with fire-arms!" Yet he honored him as a gallant soldier. Perceiving that the time had come when Northerners and Southerners could speak of these things with perfect calmness, I was glad to respond to the spirit thus manifested, in giving a picture of General Sherman as I saw him last. It was at the funeral of General Grant. In that last tribute of respect I was permitted to take part, having been requested to represent the Presbyterians, as Bishop Potter represented the Episcopalians, and we rode together. In the second carriage behind us sat General Sheridan with General Buckner; side by side with whom (for the carriages moved in double column) were General Sherman and General Joseph E. Johnston, the two chieftains who twenty-two years ago were opposed to each other in the battles which raged round this very city of Atlanta. All along Broadway and Fifth avenue, a distance of miles, the streets were black with human beings, hushed and silent as they saw pass by the catafalque on which rested the body of our great soldier; and when at the close of the day the doors of the mausoleum swung open, and he was laid to rest, while a group of warriors stood round with uncovered heads, all felt that the strife and the bitterness of the past were buried in that honored grave.

In the procession of that day rode a Southern officer, of whom (as his home is here in Atlanta) it seems not inappropriate to tell a story in harmony with the spirit of the hour. As it has been related to me by *both* the actors in the scene described, I can vouch for its literal accuracy. I give it as nearly as I can in the very words of that gallant soldier of Georgia, General John B. Gordon:

" It was the first day of Gettysburg. The battle was in progress when I came into it with my division, and struck the Federal line at an angle, which caused it to break, doubling on itself, so that it was driven back in some disorder. As it was retreating, and our line advancing, in crossing a field I saw an officer lying on the ground, and dismounted to see if I could render him any assistance. Raising him up, the blood spurted from him, and I thought that he must be mortally wounded. To my inquiry for his name, he answered that he was General Barlow of New York.* I asked him if I could be of any service to him. He said ' No,' and told me to leave him and go and do my duty. But on my pressing the offer of assistance, he asked me to send word to his wife, who was in the rear of General Meade's army. I answered that I would not only send *to* her, but send *for* her. I called for bearers, who were coming on the field to pick up the wounded, to bring a stretcher. They took him up and carried him back to ' the branch ' (the name given at the South to a stream), on which a camp hospital had been improvised; and I sent an aid with a flag of truce to the lines to forward the message to the wife of the wounded and, as I supposed, dying officer. The message reached its destination, although Mrs. Barlow was seventeen miles back from the front, and at two o'clock in the morning word was brought to me that she was at the lines. I sent word to have her immediately passed through, but bade the messenger tell her that her

---

* An officer of whom we heard a great deal during the war, as his courage made him always seek the place of danger, so that it was not uncommon after a battle to see his name reported with the brief announcement: " Wounded as usual!"

husband was 'desperately wounded.' I had no idea that she would find him alive.

"The next morning the battle was resumed, and all that had passed was forgotten in the great struggle. It was nearly two years more to the close of the war. I remained in the army to the last, and was with General Lee when he surrendered at Appomattox. When all was over I returned home to help restore the fortunes of my State. if anything were left to her in the general ruin. Years passed on, and I was chosen United States Senator from Georgia. When in Washington, I was invited one evening to dine at Mr. Clarkson N. Potter's. I did not arrive till the guests were seated. Among the others to whom I was introduced I heard the name of Barlow, but took no notice of it till there was a pause in the conversation, when I turned to the gentleman so designated and said, 'Pray, sir, may I ask if you are a relative of the General Barlow who was killed at Gettysburg?' Imagine my astonishment at the answer: 'I am the man!' 'And you, sir,' he asked in reply—'are you the General Gordon who picked me up on the field?' I could not deny it. At this he sprang to his feet, and I thought would have leaped over the table. And then he told the story of the scene in which we had met before, at which not only the ladies, but the men round the table, found it difficult to control their emotion."

How can officers who have met thus on the field of battle ever regard each other but with manly affection? And can we of the North ever look upon men who have shown such qualities as "enemies"? On the contrary, we claim them as our friends and brothers, and would defend them with our lives.

It was nearly eleven o'clock when we rose from the table only to renew, with many a warm grasp of the hand, the expressions of mutual regard. Half an hour later, we were on our way to Chattanooga.

III.

CHATTANOOGA—THE TOWN AND THE BATTLE—THE CHARGE
OF CLEBURNE AT CHICKAMAUGA—COAL AND IRON
IN THE TENNESSEE MOUNTAINS—SOUTH PITTSBURG—
MURFREESBORO—THIRTY THOUSAND GRAVES.

IT is one of the infelicities of " travelling in state," with
a special train, that we undertake to do too much, and are
whirled about from point to point without seeing many
things which we could see if we took it more deliberately.
It was toward midnight when we left Atlanta, and at day-
break were at Chattanooga—an easy way of getting over
the distance; but just here we should have been quite willing to go more slowly and in the clear light of day, for this
is historic ground. In these few hours we had passed over
the scene of the great campaign of Sherman in 1864, ending with the capture of Atlanta and the March to the Sea.
A book has recently appeared entitled " A Horseback Ride
from Chattanooga to Atlanta," written by one who took
this means of revisiting the scenes of great events in which
he had taken part. He might well spend weeks and
months in riding slowly over ground where every day he
came upon the scene of a battle. That memorable Summer these hills blazed with camp-fires for more than a
hundred miles. As I lay awake, recalling these events,
which are not even yet so far distant, I realized more than
ever the change which had come over the scene! The moon
was shedding her tranquil light on a land in perfect peace.
Instead of the booming of guns, which then woke the
echoes of these hills, not a sound was heard save the rushing of streams, or the moaning of the wind through the

forest. Blessed stillness! better than all the pomp and magnificence of war. And blessed peace! the benediction of God upon the world.

In the morning our car was standing in a net-work of tracks, which marks the entrance of different roads to this great railway center. The first peep out of the window showed the outline of Lookout Mountain, on the top of which Hooker fought above the clouds; and as soon as we could step to the end of the car, before us lay the whole line of Missionary Ridge, which was held by Bragg's army until it was driven from it in the tremendous charge of Grant at the Battle of Chattanooga.

Very soon familiar faces began to appear, for, as it was known that we were coming, the friends of Mr. Inman (who are numerous here as everywhere at the South) were on hand to greet us. With my eagerness to know every-thing, I began to ask questions about the points of historic interest. Our time was limited, as we had another place to visit during the day, and were to be in Nashville at night; but I was determined to see what I could in two or three hours, and as soon as we could despatch breakfast, carriages were waiting for us. Cameron Hill, which rises above the town, furnishes the finest point of view, and to this we directed our course. The streets were deep in mud, but we went splashing through them, as if we heard a call to battle and must be in at the fray. It is over a mile even to the foot of the hill, from which it rises like a cone in an ascent that is somewhat difficult for carriages. Impatient at the slow progress, I pushed open the door, and, leaping out, bounded up the hill as fast as my legs could carry me, and was soon on the top, when, looking back, I saw my companions at the bottom of the hill—on foot, indeed, but moving very slowly, as if they feared that a battery of Con-federate artillery might open upon them. In the presence of such danger it was wonderful to see the calmness and steadiness with which this Heavy Brigade advanced up the hill, and at length carried the position without the loss of a man! No doubt it was a hard pull for them, but the view was worth it. Seldom have I seen in this country, or in any country, a position commanding a more extensive or beautiful panorama. As the hill slopes on every side, there is nothing to intercept the view, and a single sweep of the eye takes in the whole horizon. The configuration of the place is remarkable: it seems as if formed by nature to be the scene of military operations, as it is a natural fortress—a valley girdled with a circumvallation of hills. The effect of this mighty amphitheatre is heightened by the broad band of silver running through it. The Tennessee, which flows along the base of Cameron Hill, so near that it seems as if we could throw a pebble into it, does not take a straight course through the valley, but winds about as if it had tried to force a passage in every direction, and, being driven back, had turned like a lion at bay, till finally it had broken through in the distance, and rolled away to the North, to empty itself at last into the Ohio.

I had the good fortune to have in the carriage with me two Confederate officers (indeed, to confess the truth, I looked out for this in the first place) who had been in the Battle of Chattanooga, and could speak of it as eye-witnesses. So, as we stood on the top of the hill, I said to one of them: "Now give me the points of compass and the position of the armies." "Well," he answered, "you see across the river yonder a ridge covered with trees. That way the Federals came. Though we knew that they were approaching, yet at last they appeared suddenly. I remember the first shell that fell in Chattanooga. It was on Thanksgiving-day in 1863. The people were in church. I am sorry to say I was differently employed. Henry Watterson—now of "The Courier Journal" of Louisville—and I were editing a little paper called "The Chattanooga Rebel."

Instead of being in church, as we ought to have been, we were playing cards when from the forest beyond the river came the booming of a gun, and the shell seemed to burst over our heads. *We did not stop to finish the game!*" Whether the unaccustomed sound gave a lurid turn to his editorials afterward, he did not say; though I believe "The Rebel" continued to appear, whistling to keep its courage up, until "the Yankees" became rather numerous, and it concluded that discretion was the better part of valor, and Chattanooga knew it no more.

"Did you see anything more of the war?"

"Yes, indeed: here," pointing to an ugly scar on his face, "is the mark of a shot which one of your boys gave me as they charged up Missionary Ridge." I must say that my companion spoke of this little incident with perfect good nature (a soldier is generally proud of his wounds), looking upon it as a kind of "love-tap"—a gentle touch which some sharpshooter had given him "just to remember him by." It is very pleasant to see how the men of both sides talk of these things without a particle of resentment. Like the brave fellows they were, since they were in war, they learned to take it as it came—its ups and downs, its fortunes and misfortunes, its victories and defeats; and now that it is all over, they speak of it only with the interest which they must feel in recounting the most eventful period of their lives.

Returning to our car, we found other friends waiting for us, who entertained us for the half hour before our departure with experiences, not of war, but of politics and elections. Judge Bradford told a good story of a campaign which he had made among the mountains of Eastern Tennessee. An election is a great event for the people of the country round, who look forward to it as they would to a circus, where they are to have a varied entertainment. Sometimes the young people, taking advantage of the miscellaneous gathering, have a dance under the trees; and if a politician were to frown upon them, he would probably lose his election. Imagine, then, the consternation of the Judge when he arrived on the ground, to find that the fiddler was drunk! "But," he said, "as good luck would have it, in his early days he had learned to play on the violin; and taking it in his hands, he played with such vigor that, though it was a district which polled between four and five hundred votes, *he got every vote*, and was triumphantly elected!"

As we resumed our ride, my thoughts went back to the war. It was impossible to banish it from our minds, near as we were to the scene of great events. In the group seated in the saloon of the car was a gentleman a little over forty years of age, of very manly appearance, to whom I was introduced as Major Baxter of Nashville. The military title led me to inquire if he, too, had taken part in these stirring scenes. He answered very modestly as to himself, not wishing to magnify anything he had done (though I learned from others that he had been a very brave and gallant officer), yet he was willing to give me any information. I found that he was but a boy when the war broke out, and had run away from his father's house, and enlisted in a company of artillery, and was afterward put in command of a battery. He had been at one time attached to the cavalry of Forrest, who was his ideal of an officer, and often accompanied him in his daring exploits. He had once been taken prisoner, and had tried to be exchanged by slipping in unnoticed among the privates, but was discovered before the exchange took place, and ordered out of the ranks, to be reserved for a different treatment—a circumstance which put him for a few hours in a painful uncertainty as to his fate. However, he was afterward exchanged and returned to the army. He was in the Battle of Chickamauga, but said, as others so often tell us, that it is impossible for a soldier or an officer, whose duties detain him in one part of the field, to get a general idea of what is going on in a battle which extends over many miles.

One incident had remained in his recollection as the most brilliant that he had ever seen in war. The field of Chickamauga is about ten miles from Chattanooga. The battle had been raging all day, and the right of our army had been defeated, and was retreating toward Chattanooga, which left the whole force of Bragg's army free to sweep round to our left, where General Thomas was holding his position with a stubborn resistance, against which the Confederates dashed themselves in vain. Again and again they had been brought up to the attack, only to be mowed down by the Federal cannon. It was late in the afternoon, and they hesitated to advance again in the face of this withering fire. A council of war was held in front of his battery, which was just in the rear of the line, at which he counted thirteen generals. The army had been fighting for hours, and some thought that it was better to withdraw, and let the troops rest till morning before the battle was resumed. But at last it was decided that General Cleburne should make one more attempt. Instantly he drew up his division in line of battle with as much precision as if they were on parade, riding along the line to see if every man was in his place. When the signal was given to charge, they rushed forward with a yell. For a few minutes all knowledge of what was going on was lost in the roar of battle. Then suddenly it seemed as if the woods were full of Federal soldiers—whether flying or advancing to attack, he could not tell—and his men stood to their guns. But it soon appeared that the charge of Cleburne had broken the line, and the Confederates camped on the ground which Thomas had held during the day.

Of course this was an exact and literal account of that part of the battle which my informant saw, although the result could not have been so great as he at the moment supposed; for, though a part of our line was broken, this did not involve a general defeat of Thomas, who held his wing of the army firmly together, and brought it safely from the field.

I was the more interested in this account because I had once had a very minute description of the battle from General Garfield, who was Rosecrans's chief of staff; and who, after the defeat of our right wing, instead of following his chief back into Chattanooga, turned his horse's head toward the sound of the cannon, and rode at full speed to join General Thomas, who was holding his own against fearful odds. General Garfield told me how magnificently that great soldier saved the day. I shall never forget his description of the opportune arrival of General Gordon Granger, who, hearing the sound of the guns, marched without orders, and came on the field at a critical moment. The particulars of this I afterward had from General Granger himself, so that I felt that I was pretty well informed about the Battle of Chickamauga; but I was glad to have this account from Major Baxter, as it threw still another side-light on one of the great battles of the war, and showed how desperately both armies fought on that terrible day.

While listening to these details, our special train was going at full speed, flying away from the scene of this great struggle at the rate of forty miles an hour; and still we were on the same trail, over which both armies passed, marching and fighting. Some years before the war Chattanooga had been chosen as the point of meeting of the railroads which connect Tennessee and Georgia; and so it became an all-important military position, since the road that passed through it was the great artery on which the Union army must depend both for re-enforcements and supplies. Hence the order of Grant to Thomas, after the disastrous Battle of Chickamauga, to "hold Chattanooga at all hazards." The President of the Railroad Company (Major Thomas), who came down from Nashville to meet us, wa in its service at the time; and as we stood at the end o_ the car, he told me how he followed the Confederate army when it retreated, putting a red flag at every bridge as a signal that it was to be destroyed, to hold in check the pursuit of the Federals, who had to stop at every stream till they built a new bridge across it.

But here is something better than war. "Look here, Doctor," said the Major, "I will show you the highest school-house in the United States;" and as we whirled round a bend of the road, he pointed upward, and craning our necks, I spied indeed a school-house perched on a peak which rose high above us. As it was painted white, it could be seen far and near, as if it had been placed there to serve as a light-house on the top of the mountains. It was a picturesque object, standing among the rocks and pines; though where the children could come from to fill it, it might puzzle one to discover. But the building itself was a sign of human habitation like one of those shelters on the High Alps, which show where the shepherd feeds his flock. More than that, it was like a chapel or a cross, such as I have seen at some high point of the Alps: a sign that where men live, there is care, not only for the body, but for the mind and soul — a reflection which gave a pleasant turn to our thoughts from the dark memories of war.

And now comes another welcome sign of industry and peace. We had been hastening our speed, that we might find time to stop at some works belonging to the Tennessee Coal and Iron and Railroad Company, in which Mr. Inman is interested. Shooting off by a side-road, we came in sight of the place, where the tall chimneys, pouring out a volume of flame and smoke, showed that the works were on a large scale. As we arrived, one of the furnaces had just made a large casting, and the iron, though still red-hot, was slowly

cooling in the moulds; and now another furnace was
opened, and the molten mass poured from it, like one
of the streams of lava from the crater of Vesuvius—a river
of fire, which is presently divided into thirty or forty
streams, and these into other smaller rivulets. And now,
reader, do you know what gives the name to pig-iron? You
have but to stand here a moment to see. As you observe
how the stream flows through long and wide channels,
from which it is diverted into the lesser ones, you see
how naturally these small moulds, supplied from the larger,
suggest the idea of so many little pigs drawing sustenance
from the maternal breast. In this case the mother has a
large litter, two or three hundred, and must have a corresponding reservoir to supply her numerous progeny. The
workmen were negroes, and as their black faces were
grimed with sweat and coal, and yet glowing with excitement, as they were lighted up by the reflection from the
hot iron, they looked like imps of darkness sporting with
infernal fires. The sight took me back to the time of the
war, when I visited the Water Shops in Springfield, Mass.,
which were kept going day and night for the manufacture
of arms. What a Vulcan's Cave that was! It seemed an
under-world, where the fires were ever burning, and the
hammers rang with a ceaseless clang. Much more pleasant
was it now to see workmen, not forging weapons of war,
but moulding bars of iron, which were to be turned into
plowshares and pruning-hooks, or into the rails over which
are to roll the wheels of civilization.

The owners of these iron-works have given the place the
rather ambitious name of South Pittsburg, although in
time it may prove itself a not unworthy child of such a
mother. In the development of new industries at the
South, nothing is more worthy of notice than the increased
production of coal and iron. For years the Great Valley
was supplied with coal from Pittsburg, which was floated

down the Ohio and Mississippi.   Much still comes that
way.   But the mountains of Tennessee are full of mines of
coal, which need only to be developed to be a source of very
great wealth.   Indeed in one particular Pittsburg itself is
very much surpassed by *South* Pittsburg, viz.: in the close
proximity of coal and iron.   These works are at the outlet
of a little valley, on one side of which are thick strata of
coal, and on the other rich beds of iron ore; so that it is an
easy matter to bring them down to the same point, where
the coal, converted into coke, can be used to melt the ore
which is converted into iron bars.   And South Pittsburg
has equal advantages with its namesake on the Ohio, in
that it is on the banks of the Tennessee, whose broad current will float the products of its mines and its furnaces to
every portion of the Great Valley.

But in Tennessee, (which was "the dark and bloody
ground" of the war almost as much as Virginia, as in it
were fought four of the greatest battles—Shiloh and Murfreesboro, Chickamauga and Chattanooga) we are constantly passing from one thing to another—from war to peace,
and from peace to war.   As we left the flaming furnaces of
South Pittsburg, we turned westward, coming out of the
hills into the more open country of Middle Tennessee, and
in the afternoon passed over the field of Murfreesboro (or
Stone River, as the battle is sometimes called, from having
been fought on its banks), where it raged for two days, and
was both lost and won.   It was begun on the last day of
the year 1862.   That day the battle went against us, though
the result was not decisive.   The next day the armies rested,
as if not willing to stain the new-born year with scenes of
blood; but on the 2d of January, 1863, the battle was resumed, and was fiercer and deadlier than before.   At one
moment the day seemed to be lost: the Union forces were
driven back by the furious charge of the Confederates;
when suddenly the tide was turned by the masterly move-

ment of Rosecrans in concentrating his artillery at one
point, which swept the field, and covered it with the dying
and the dead.   Seldom have more horrors been piled upon
a battle-plain.   One shudders to think of the agonies of
that field when the darkness fell upon it, and the rain began to pour, as if the skies were as pitiless and cruel as
man could be to man.   All that Winter night the wounded
of both armies were exposed to the fury of the elements,
their mingled groans ascending to heaven.   The very memory of those days seems to hover as a black cloud over the
peaceful landscape; but the anguish of the dying was long
since stilled, and here they sleep the sleep of "the unreturning brave."   The National Cemetery is said to contain
thirty thousand graves (!), though I can hardly believe that
the number is so great, as there are less than seventeen
thousand at Vicksburg.   But we need not be exact in the
matter: the total is fearful enough in either case.   A glance
of the eye as we swept past showed that the grounds are extensive, many acres being dotted with low headstones, each
of which marks "a soldier's sepulchre."   If those who
sleep here were to rise from their graves, as in the vision of
the Apocalypse, they would "stand up upon the earth an
exceeding great army."   God grant that our country may
never behold such scenes again!

It was dark when we reached Nashville; but, as usual,
friends were waiting for us with carriages, and we were
soon enjoying the light and warmth of a most comfortable
Hotel.

IV.

THE CITY OF NASHVILLE—GOVERNOR BATE AND EX-GOV-
ERNOR MARKS—VANDERBILT AND FISK UNIVERSITIES
—MRS. PRESIDENT POLK—VISIT TO BELLE MEADE—
FIRST AND LAST IMPRESSIONS.

As I am an old traveller, I often amuse myself in comparing my opinion of a place when I enter it with that
when I leave it: there is sometimes a wide contrast between
the first impression and the last. Thus my first glimpse
of Nashville was not attractive. We arrived just at evening, when it was no longer daylight; and yet it was not
dark enough for the lamps to be lighted, which give an
artificial brightness to city streets. A mist had come up
from the river as dense as a London fog, and as we rode to
our hotel, we could see neither to the right nor left. The
air was damp and chilly, and the outlook dreary enough;
and if we had passed through the city without stopping
(like some English travellers, who still feel competent to
give their impressions of the country), we should have said
that it was a forlorn and wretched place.

But we halted on our journey, and spent about thirty
hours in Nashville; and in that time we "walked about
Zion," and found it surrounded by a country of great natural beauty: we stood on the marble steps of the Capitol,
and took in the proportions of a very considerable city; we
visited two Universities, so that we found it was not desti-
tute of institutions of learning; and lastly, were entertained
with such generous hospitality, that we came to the conclu-
sion that it had a distinguished society. That my readers
may share in the pleasures of that happy day, I must take

them with us in our rides as in our receptions, that they may appreciate the pleasant memories that linger on the banks of the Cumberland.

Hardly had we entered the Maxwell House before we were informed that some of the good people of the place had had the kind thought to give us a dinner that very evening; and as soon as we could go to our rooms, and make a hurried preparation, we were ushered into a large parlor, to find the Governor of Tennessee waiting to receive us, with a number of gentlemen who are generally designated by the reporters as "prominent citizens," and soon filed into a dining-room, where the pleasant company was seated round a long table, with Governor Bate at one end and ex-Governor Marks at the other. It was my good fortune to have a seat by the latter—a gentleman of great intelligence, who had been identified with the history of the State in peace and war. He gave me gratifying information of the condition of the South, which showed that its recovery, though slow, was steady, and promised a long career of prosperity.

But I was still more interested in some personal reminiscences, to which (as he referred to them in a speech in the course of the evening) it may not be overstepping the limits of modesty for me to allude.

At the close of the war, the North and the South were both in a state of great irritation. Though their hostility could no longer vent itself in open combat, it was pent up in millions of hearts that were full of bitterness. The North had suffered terribly in her homes; her sons were lying on a hundred battle-fields, and she was in no mood for leniency toward those who had brought upon the land such immeasurable woes. Some, forgetting the wise saying of Burke, that "you can not frame an indictment of treason against a whole people," would have had the Confederate leaders tried by court-martial, with the full penalty of treason. Some were enraged that General Lee was allowed to escape punishment. It is even said that Secretary Stanton once issued an order for his arrest, that he might be brought before a military tribunal. It is one of the thousand things we owe to General Grant that by his firmness he saved the country from a great infamy. General Lee had surrendered on the field of battle, and was entitled to the protection given to a prisoner of war; and General Grant felt that his own personal honor as a soldier, as well as the honor of the country, were involved in keeping faith with him. We can now see the wisdom as well as the justice of such moderation. General Lee, the leader of the Confederate armies, became the great pacificator of the South. Retiring to his home in Lexington, and remaining there in quiet dignity, he gave an example of moderation and self-restraint which did more than any other man's could have done for the restoration of good feeling between the North and South. Had the Government touched a hair of his head, it would have left in the Southern heart a hatred that would have been perpetuated from generation to generation.

Thus the fury of passion was baffled in one way, but only to show itself in another. Failing to establish military tribunals, it resorted to a vindictive legislation, which we can hardly believe to have been in existence in our day. Congress passed a test-oath aimed especially at lawyers, who were supposed to have taken a very active part in stirring up the Rebellion. By this all attorneys and counsellors-at-law were required, before they could resume the practice of their profession, to swear that they had had nothing to do with the Rebellion. The effect of this can be imagined in a community where almost every able-bodied man had been in the ranks of the army. It outlawed hundreds and thousands of the most capable men in the Southern States. Governor Marks told me how it bore upon his own case. He said: "I came out of the war ruined. I had a wife and child. What could I do for their support?

I had not the trade of a mechanic; I could not be a carpenter or a blacksmith; I could not even be a laborer" (he had lost a leg on the battle-field); "I could only practice my profession—that of the law—and that I was forbidden to do. That test-oath was a decree of starvation—a sentence of death."

Yet such was the temper of the people that this monstrous legislation was not only enacted by Congress, but to a large extent approved and sustained by public opinion at the North. And I remember well when a certain Judge (whose name was brought up in this conversation), who had been appointed by Lincoln, was said to have "gone back" on the Union sentiment of the North, because he differed from some of his colleagues in his conviction that, since the war was over, it was time that martial law should cease, and that confiscation and outlawry should come to an end. Yet there was the law, in the statutes of the United States, to be rigidly enforced until it could in some legitimate way be annulled. Congress would not repeal it. There remained but one hope of relief—in the Supreme Court of the United States, which might declare the law unconstitutional; and on that august tribunal nearly one-half the Judges were in favor of sustaining these test-oaths. They were condemned only by a majority of one, and I was proud to think that one of my name and kindred took an active part in that decision, and wrote the opinion of the Court. It never came home to me before as it did now, when I had before me an illustration of its effect. "That decision," said Governor Marks, "set me free; my limbs were unbound. From that moment I could enter the courts and practice my profession." And he did practice it so well that he rose not only to the front rank at the bar, but to such public respect and importance that he was elected Governor of the State. His face flushed as he spoke of the bitter time when he was left with nothing under heaven but his wife and child, and was prohibited even from using his voice or his brain for their support; and his heart warmed toward me in grateful remembrance of an act of justice once performed by my brother.

As he spoke thus of one who was very dear to me, I told him that the Judge lived in a house which had a historic interest. When Washington was taken by the British troops in 1814, and the Capitol was burned, there was an immediate pressure for the removal of the seat of government to some other city. To prevent this, the leading citizens of Washington purchased a lot and erected upon it (at a cost of $30,000) a building for the temporary accommodation of Congress. It was completed December 4th, 1815, and immediately leased at an annual rent of $1650, and here the legislative sessions were held until the Capitol was rebuilt and ready for occupation. Here Henry Clay presided as Speaker of the House of Representatives. In front of the building James Monroe was inaugurated President with great brilliancy March 4, 1817. When the Capitol was so far rebuilt that the two Houses could occupy their chambers in it their late quarters were turned into a fashionable boarding-house, which was the home of many Senators and Representatives when they were in Washington, including Daniel Webster and John C. Calhoun, and here the latter breathed his last.

Later still, it went through another transformation. When the late war came on, as it was Government property, it might have been turned into soldiers' barracks—a convenient place for a guard of the public buildings. Instead of that it was put to another use—in being converted into a Military Prison. This was the Old Capitol Prison, of which we heard so much during the war, as the place in which so many Southern officers were confined. After the war, being no longer needed for any kind of military occupation, it was sold by Congress, and purchased by the Sergeant-at-Arms of the Senate, who put a mansard roof upon it, and converted it into three beautiful private residences, one of which is owned by Mr. Evarts, one by General Dunn, and the other (which is at the end of the row, and has a large extension for a library, with open grounds) by Judge Field, who, as he is given to hospitality, often welcomes to it his Southern friends, some of whom, as they enter his charming home, look round with a quiet smile, and tell him that they have on a former occasion had the honor of a residence within those walls, but in circumstances not quite so agreeable as those in which they now find themselves!

While we were enjoying this quiet conversation, Governor Bate, who had the rest of our party around him at the other end of the table, was keeping them in a roar with his stories. He, too, had been in the war, and was one of General Hood's division commanders in the battle of Franklin, and the longer conflict around the city of Nashville. He is a man of fine presence, and carries himself with a military air, standing erect like a grenadier. Not the least of his military qualities is a certain gayety of manner, which belongs to the dashing soldier. He has a very pleasing address, and when he rose to speak, he and his friend, Col. Colyar, of "The Nashville Union," by their interchange of wit, kept us all in a merry mood; while Governor Marks, if he spoke in a somewhat graver tone, added not less to the general satisfaction by his words, which were so cordial, and so manly and patriotic.

The next morning I was "abroad," as usual, at an early hour, arm in arm with Col. Colyar, who kindly took me through the principal streets, which show that Nashville is a place of importance commercially as well as politically, as a center of business for the Middle South, as well as the capital of the great State of Tennessee. Among other large buildings, I espied the Publishing House of the Cum-

berland Presbyterian Church, and immediately entered to
introduce myself, and take the hands of the excellent
brethren, who are our spiritual kindred, and whom we
hope some day to welcome into a closer fellowship of the
saints in an organic union of all who hold substantially the
same faith, in one Holy, Catholic, and Apostolic Presbyterian Church of the United States of America.

Returning to the hotel we found carriages waiting to
take us to Vanderbilt University, which is a mile or so
from the city. The country around Nashville is rolling,
offering in its numerous elevations many beautiful sites for
public buildings. As soon as we were out of town I kept
a sharp lookout for some memorial of the great battle
which had once raged over these hills; but almost every
trace of it had disappeared. Here and there might be seen
a low earthwork which had once been grim with the
mouths of cannon frowning over it, but now not a gun was
to be seen anywhere. The very works themselves had been
almost washed away by rains, leaving only a few grassy
mounds over which children may play in these happy times
of peace.

We soon rode into a large inclosure that swells upward to
a considerable elevation, and is crested with the stately
buildings of Vanderbilt University. The campus is of
many acres in extent, which are set out with trees. The
good Methodist Bishop, who is President of the Institution,
has a passion for trees, and has collected within the grounds
a very great number and variety of those which are native
to this part of the country. When these have attained
their growth, here will be one of the grandest collections of
American trees on the continent, showing the richness and
variety of the Southern forests. The President, whose
portly form we had recognized coming across the lawn,
now met us, and we went up the steps together. As we
stood at the top of the long flight, and looked around, it

seemed as if a more beautiful site could not have been chosen. The view extends over the country for miles. Though in full view of the city, this hill-top is far enough away not to be disturbed by any sound from its streets; it has that quiet and stillness which are needed in an institution of learning. In the chapel, where the students meet for morning and evening prayers, is a full-length portrait of Commodore Vanderbilt, who gave a million of dollars to found the University; and a smaller one of his wife, whose sweet face appears here with the utmost propriety, as it is commonly believed that the generous gift of her husband was due to her gentle inspiration. There is also a portrait of the late William H. Vanderbilt, who added a quarter of a million to the endowment. Such an institution (if it be recognized by the family as the monument of their father and grandfather, for which the sons and grandsons are to care) will never want for money. But something more than money is needed to make a great University; and of this intellectual provision we find proofs in the library, and recitation-rooms and laboratories, and in the faces of the Professors, to whom we were introduced. This excellent corps of teachers, furnished with these noble halls and every facility for academic training, give promise that Vanderbilt University, though as yet in its youth, will live for generations, and be immensely useful in the long career to which it is destined.

Returning to the front, as our eyes swept round the circuit of the hills, we descried in another direction Fisk University; and though it required us to make a considerable detour, we could not go away without visiting an institution of which we had heard so much. Major Baxter was in the carriage with me, and as we rode along pointed to a gloomy building where he had been a prisoner for a short time during the war, unable to communicate with his family who were so near! But we dismiss these memories as we ride up to Fisk University, which, like Vanderbilt, stands on a hill overlooking the city. This was one of the first institutions for the colored people established after the war, and took its name from Gen. Clinton B. Fisk, who had always been a friend of the negro as he has been of the Indian, and whose large and kindly face looks upon us from the walls. Here President Cravath received us very warmly, and, after showing us through the building, took us to Jubilee Hall, so called because erected with money earned by the Jubilee Singers, who have sung their plaintive melodies in the cities of this country and in Europe, where they have been listened to with interest by audiences of the highest rank, not only in Great Britain, but on the Continent; even those who could not understand their language recognizing in the pathos of their songs the echo of a mournful history. It was a beautiful thought to use their marvellous gift of music for the benefit of the institution to which they owed so much, by which they gave delight to tens of thousands of hearers in two continents, and at the same time rendered a lasting service to their race.

Both these buildings are large, and the rooms for study and recitation as spacious as in a New England College. In the library was a pure African, the son of a chief, who hopes, when he completes his education, to return to his native country. Who can tell what a future may be his? He may be a messenger of Christianity and of civilization to his countrymen on the coast, and in the forests and along the rivers of Africa! President Cravath wished us to wait till he could assemble the students for some public exercises. But as we had another engagement, our time was very brief; yet brief as it was, it gave us some impressions which we shall long retain. It was very cheering to get even a glimpse of so many bright, intelligent countenances; to see how freedom has brought a new light into those dark African faces, as it has brought sunshine into their lives. Long may they live to sing, not the songs of bondage, but of deliverance!

Our visit was hastened by an appointment which we had to pay our respects to the wife of President Polk, who is still living in the home to which they came on his retirement from the Presidency thirty-seven years since, and where he died, and in front of which he is buried. Entering the drawing-room, we found standing to receive us one who seemed the very ideal of "a lady of the old school," with manners a little stately, but extremely gracious—the combination best befitting one of the exalted station that she occupied forty years ago, which then captivated all who saw her in the midst of the throng in the White House, and which still lend a charm to her advancing years.

Major Thomas welcomed us in her name, and after we had been presented, one of our party, who was asked to reply, referred first of all to her illustrious husband, whose name has such a place in an important period of American history, as the four years of his administration included the war with Mexico and the acquisition of California, and from it dates the existence of our Pacific Empire. He then expressed for himself and his associates the great pleasure they all felt in being permitted to pay their respects to one who united in herself two generations, and their wishes for her continued happiness, in which he was sure he but reflected the wishes of the whole American people.

One more visit of state—to the Governor in the Capitol; and then we betook ourselves to the home of Major Baxter, where we were entertained with true Southern hospitality. Three o'clock found us again at the station, where a special train was waiting to take us a few miles into the country, to one of the most famous stock farms in the South—Belle Meade, the home of General Jackson, a brother of the United States Senator. The park is extensive and beautiful, with deer feeding under the ancient trees. Here are bred the most famous race-horses in the country. The General would think it almost a degradation if one of his horses were harnessed to a carriage. We were shown a great number of colts, graceful as fawns, which are expected to bring large prices at the annual sale in April. Though I could not appreciate the peculiar fineness of limb and shoulder which made them of such value, it needed but a common eye to perceive their exceeding grace and beauty.

Then we were taken to see the kings of the turf, that had won innumerable victories on the most famous courses in this country and in England—horses that had a pedigree reaching back, it seemed to me, to the pair that came out of the Ark. As the General indicated with enthusiasm their special "points," which made them superior to all other horses in the world, I tried to look wise, and nodded my head approvingly, though in my heart I was obliged to confess that he could not have found a person more ignorant on the subject in the State of Tennessee. I tell my friend, Mr. Robert Bonner, that I have a horse up in the country for which I paid a hundred and seventy-five dollars, which I would not exchange for Maud S., for which he paid forty thousand! "My faithful creature keeps an even pace, is straightforward and steady-going—'a regular Presbyterian'—not to be confounded with your jumpers and flyers, that go over the ground like a flash of lightning"—at which he laughs heartily at my simplicity.

The hospitalities of the day ended with a dinner in the evening at a private house, which brought together a number of gentlemen, who formed a most agreeable company; and when at eleven o'clock we returned to our hotel, we all felt that we had seldom had the good fortune to find ourselves in a more delightful city than Nashville, so widely did our last impression differ from the first.

At midnight we were on our way to Alabama.

V.

DOWN IN ALABAMA—THE BATTLE OF FRANKLIN—BIRMING-
HAM—" PEACE, PIG-IRON, AND PROSPERITY "—MONT-
GOMERY, THE CRADLE OF THE CONFEDERACY—GOVER-
NOR O'NEAL.

EVERY morning we wake up in a new State. One day it is Georgia; then it is Tennessee; and now it is Alabama. If any of my readers should take the map to follow us, he would see that we took a zig-zag course: first bearing South by West to Atlanta; then North by West to Chattanooga and Nashville; and now South again to Birmingham and Montgomery. These crooks and turns are merely eccen-tricities of genius—little diversions from the regular routes, which are nothing to those who have all power to go whither and how they will. With a special train at our command, we care little about latitude and longitude: dis-tances are nothing. We can make an appointment to breakfast a hundred miles away, as easily as in the country I could walk across the lawn to breakfast with my nearest neighbor.

But except as a matter of convenience, to reach certain points at a designated hour, I could wish that we were not whirled about quite so fast, and that we made our journeys in broad daylight, instead of

> " Folding our tents like the Arabs,
> And silently stealing away "

in the darkness of the night; for here, as in coming from Atlanta to Chattanooga, we are on historic ground. Only eighteen miles south of Nashville, we pass through Frank-

lin, which recalls one of the most desperate battles of the
war. It is an old story, but an old story becomes new when
you hear it, as I did, from the lips of one who was in the
scene, and tells his own personal experiences. How the
battle came to be fought at all, is one of the remarkable
incidents of a war abounding in surprises. A word will explain the military situation.

The fall of Atlanta, Sept. 2, 1864, left Sherman in possession of that strategic point, but at a long distance from
his base. He had to depend on the North for supplies, the
greater part of which came through Louisville, five hundred miles away, every mile of which had to be guarded.
This long line was his weak point, the one most exposed to
attack. Unable to drive back the invader by direct assault,
Hood determined to get in his rear, and cut his communi-
cations. Since Sherman had invaded Georgia, he would
invade Tennessee. This was one of the critical moments
in war, which it is the part of military genius to seize and
turn to advantage. Seeing his purpose, Sherman, instead
of opposing it, permitted him to carry it out; indeed he
helped him in it by tearing up the rails for miles in the
rear of his army, to cut off pursuit as he struck through
Georgia. At the same time he sent Thomas to Nashville
to hold that vital point, and despatched two corps under
Schofield to support him, while he undertook his great
march to the sea. Thus Hood was left between two armies,
not closing in upon him, but moving in opposite directions,
and, with an infatuation which it is difficult to understand,
instead of following Sherman, and harassing his march, he
took the directly opposite course—a movement of which
General Grant says that " it seemed to be leading to his
certain doom. At all events, had I the power to command
both armies, I should not have changed the orders under
which he seemed to be acting." But Hood could not resist
the temptation to pursue Schofield (who had but seventeen

thousand men, while he had over forty thousand), whom
he hoped to overtake and destroy before he could reach
Nashville. It was a race between them. Schofield had
passed through Columbia in rapid march, the enemy in hot
pursuit. The next point which he was aiming to reach was
the village of Franklin, which lies in the bend of a little
river that sweeps round it. If he could but get his artillery
and baggage-trains safely across that river, it would afford
him a line of defence which he could hold till he could con-
tinue the march in safety. Accordingly he had sent forward a pressing message to have pontoons at that point to
construct a bridge, that he might pass over without delay.
What was his consternation at arriving to find that not a
single pontoon had been provided! Nothing remained but
to throw up hasty earthworks across the bend of the river,
and drawing his little army within it, to make his stand
there, to live or to die. The Confederates came on in force,
and attacked with the utmost fury. Braver men never
marched to battle. The events of war, as of peace, sometimes depend on very slight causes. It is said that the day
before, Hood had reproached his generals for allowing the
Federal army to escape at Spring Hill. Such reproaches
stung the proud spirit of brave men, and they went into
battle with a bitter feeling, determined to leave no chance
for reproaches hereafter. In this mood Cleburne, who
made that gallant charge at Chickamauga, led his division
into the fire, and was actually spurring his horse over the
breastworks, when horse and rider fell under a shower of
balls. His death recalls an incident of which Sam Jones
makes very effective use. It is said that the Confederate line,
as it advanced, was enfiladed by a battery planted in a grove
of the black locust-trees so common in that region. Seeing
his men cut to pieces, General Hood, who was sitting
on his horse in the rear, watching the battle, sent one
of his aids with the following order: "Give my compli-

ments to General Cleburne, and tell him that I ask at his hands the battery in the Locust Grove!" The aid disappeared, and quickly returned with the message: " General Cleburne is dead, sir." Again the commander spoke: " Give my compliments to General Adams, and tell him that I ask at his hands the battery in the Locust Grove!" Again the message is returned: " General Adams is dead, sir." Once more went the unflinching order to a third commander with the same result. The moral is evident. The thrice repeated command is meant to illustrate the duty of unquestioning obedience, and, as might be supposed, is used with startling effect on a Confederate audience, though the fiery preacher afterward introduced it in one of his great meetings in Chicago, when, after winding up his hearers to the highest pitch, he gave the word of command somewhat after this fashion: " As adjutant of the Lord of Hosts, I ask at your hands the city of Chicago: that you compel it to surrender to the Lord Jesus Christ!"—an undertaking more difficult than to storm any battery that ever hurled death into the face of a foe.

It is a pity to mar a tale that has been worked up with such thrilling effect. But it is denied by some, who look upon it as one of those legends of battle in which a slight incident is magnified by the imagination. Others, however, affirm it to be literally true. Certainly it *could* have been, for nothing was more perfectly in keeping with the heroic courage shown on that awful day.

The carnage was fearful. In those five hours (the battle began at four o'clock in the afternoon, and continued till nine, and at that season—it was the last day of November, when the sun sets before five o'clock—it was chiefly after night-fall, so that both sides could see to fire only by the flashing of each other's guns) the Confederates lost six thousand men! The number of officers killed was such as was seldom known in the war. Mr. Cunningham of " The

Nashville American " tells me that, though he was little more than a boy, he was in the ranks, and in the very front.   The first charge of the Confederates had broken our line in the center, and though they were soon driven back, they still held a portion of the breastworks; while our troops formed another line behind it.   The two were but twenty-five yards apart, and at this close range poured a murderous fire into each other.   My informant says that when he came to the ditch, it was filled with the dying and the dead, so that *he had to climb over them* to get up to the breastworks.   Those standing in the ditch loaded the rifles, and passed them up to those in front, who thus kept up a constant firing; but expected every moment, as the assault seemed hopeless, to receive an order from General Stahl, who was standing just behind them, to retreat; but the grim soldier, with German stubbornness, answered only, " Keep firing!" when he too was riddled with bullets.   As they carried him off dying, he called for his Colonel to turn over the command to him, who continued the desperate battle till he too was shot down; and (as Governor Cox of Ohio, who was in the battle, and has written the history of the campaign, tells the story) he was so walled in by the slain that he could not *fall*, and there was seen in the gray of the morning still erect, as if giving the word of command to that " bivouac of the dead!"   During all this rage of battle, this boy-soldier, whose comrades were falling every instant beside him, expected that the next minute would be his last.   How he escaped, he can not tell.   To this day a horror comes over him as he recalls that awful scene; and how he was saved

> " Out of the jaws of death,
> Out of the mouth of hell,"

is one of the mysteries of his life.

But enough of war. We can not stand much of this at
a time; and so, when we have given our readers a short
chapter, we change the subject, if it were only for the effect
of contrast. After brooding over the horrors of a battle-
field, it is a relief to get into the solemn stillness of the
woods, among " the murmuring pines and the hemlocks."
Nature is the great restorer of body and mind. The tree-
tops that wave gently over our heads, and the soft winds
that stir in the pines, whisper " Peace." Northern Alabama has great forests, dark with shadows which tempt the
imagination, and full of coverts, where the deer feed un-
scared by the rifle of the hunter. And now, as the morning advances, we find ourselves in a region where a geolo-
gist would discover, in the rocks which crop out of the
mountain sides, the evidences of vast mineral deposits. Alabama is in the South what Pennsylvania is in the North
—a State whose treasures are in the bowels of the earth, in
which she has enough buried to make the wealth of half a
dozen States. As in Eastern Tennessee, the seams of· coal
lie·in close proximity to the beds of iron ore. Here and
there we came upon a mining camp in the woods, and stopping the train, climbed up to the mouth of a shaft which
had been bored into the side of a mountain. The ore-beds
are of enormous extent, eight or ten feet thick, lying almost on a level, or at a gentle incline, so as to be easy for
mining. In one ridge along which we passed, the iron ore
is said to extend forty miles!

After a rapid survey of these treasures of the hills, we
ran down to Birmingham, of which we had heard so much
—a city which has sprung up in a night, but which has
great possibilities. Here, as usual, friends were waiting
for us with carriages to take us round the town, which is
laid out on a grand scale. The " pattern " is large.
Whether it will ever be " filled up " is another question.
But·it has made a good beginning, the long and wide streets

showing already blocks of fine buildings. The first fruit of this is a fever of speculation. A land company owns a large portion of the town, and lots are selling at prices which seem very high for a place in the woods: but as our Western cities have grown out of just such beginnings, Birmingham may go forward at the same rapid pace.

Naturally the residents of a town of so much promise, are happy to receive distinguished visitors. Not long since Mr. Randall paid them a visit, and recognizing him as the great protector of the iron industry, they wished to do him honor, and got out a military company with a cannon, and fired a salute. Of course he found them ready converts to the Pennsylvania doctrine of protection, since they had the same article to be protected. Indeed they expressed what they thought necessary to the welfare of the country by a banner mounted on the tallest smoke-stack in the town, on which were blazoned in huge letters the words " PEACE, PIG-IRON, AND PROSPERITY!"

Without indulging in any extravagance of dreamers or of speculators, it does seem to me quite within bounds to anticipate for this new " Tadmor in the Wilderness " a very remarkable growth in wealth and population; that it may become, as the center of a vast region of coal and iron, one of the IRON CITIES of the United States, or indeed of the world, like Pittsburg in this country, or its namesake, Birmingham, or Sheffield, in England.

We went off at a ringing gait, as if the iron horse had caught the breeze from the Gulf, and at three o'clock reached Montgomery. As we stepped out of the car, Mr. Inman was greeted by numerous friends (he seems to have friends everywhere), who took possession of us as their guests, and putting us in carriages, rode into the town. We had not gone far, however, before we reined up at the Exchange Hotel, and were ushered into a drawing-room, where the Governor of Alabama was standing to receive us.

He is a fine old gentleman, of military appearance: for he too (like Governor Bate of Tennessee) was a General before he was a Governor. The name of General O'Neal was familiar to us during the war as one of the hard fighters of the South. He was one of Stonewall Jackson's lieutenants, by whose side he fought through many a bloody day. But bronzed old soldier as he is, he was now the very picture of gentleness, and received us, not only politely, but with the utmost cordiality, responding warmly to the sentiment of "Liberty and Union forever!"

After these greetings, he entered one of the carriages with us, and we drove to the Capitol. This is a historic building. Montgomery was the cradle of the Confederacy, and on the porch of the Capitol Jefferson Davis took the oath of office as its President. I stood on the very stone, and can truly say that I had it *under my feet*. The Governor took us into his office, where were held the meetings of the Confederate Cabinet until the government was removed to Richmond. How different now from that time of plottings and conspiracies! The sky was clear, and the sun shone brightly on the beautiful landscape; and an hour later, from this very terrace where we were standing, was heard the firing of minute-guns in honor of General Hancock, as that gallant Union soldier was laid in his grave!

As we rode away from the Capitol, I was seated in the carriage with the Governor, and so accustomed have we become to this sort of thing (this is the third Governor—or fourth, counting ex-Governor Marks—who has received us in three days) that some of us doubt whether it will do hereafter to associate with anybody of less rank than a Governor. Perhaps we may come down to a Mayor (the Mayor here has been very civil to us); but as for associations inferior to these, they must be accepted with a certain reserve!

But whatever other courtesies you may receive, a dinner

3

is the be-all and the end-all of hospitality, so that our riding ended at the Club. As we were to leave at half-past eight for New Orleans, we sat down at six. We had a generous host to preside in Colonel John C. Graham, a well-known citizen of Montgomery, who accompanied us to New Orleans and Memphis, and added much to the pleasure of our journey. At the other end of the table sat the Governor, and as I looked at this grizzled old warrior, I recalled the scenes through which he had passed, especially that fearful day at Chancellorsville, when he rode through the fiercest storm of battle, and his soldiers expected every moment to see him fall. I am not a bit disturbed at meeting the " Confederate brigadiers," for I find them brave men, and however I dislike the cause for which they fought, I can not but appreciate their heroic courage. Recognizing this, I could say in truth, in the few words that fell to me, that much as we might mourn the calamities of war, it had at least one good effect, viz: to inspire in the combatants a profound respect for each other. It was a favorite maxim of Napoleon that " power is never ridiculous;" and war, as the most terrific exhibition of the energies of man, inspires a respect which is not always given to the highest genius or the purest virtue. When one receives a stunning blow in the forehead, he may hate him who gave it; but as he reels under it, and picks himself up, he can not despise the hand that struck him squarely. He may feel the utmost bitterness toward his adversary, but he can not feel contempt. So with great bodies of men: war sometimes teaches them what they would never learn in times of peace. Our civil war has caused the North and the South to know each other better than ever before. The North has come to respect the South—its vast resources: its power of organization, of resistance to forces that seemed overwhelming; and, above all, its courage and indomitable will.

And, on the other hand, the Southerners are quite as

ready to admit that they mistook their adversaries: that they did not understand the North before. Those whom they thought craven and cowardly, and wholly given to money-making, they have met in the field, and the shock of battle has wrought a revolution in their sentiments. They do not object to telling a story against themselves, and it is a very good one that they tell here of Judge Rice, a well-known Alabamian, who was very loud in his talk before the war, predicting that Yankees would run like sheep: "He could whip them with popguns!" When the war was over, some one reminded him of his boastful prophecy that he "would whip the Yankees with pop-guns," to which he replied with a wit that disarmed further criticism: "Yes, we *could* have whipped them with popguns, but [with an oath] *they wouldn't fight that way!*"

Now this mutual respect, which the war has done more than all preceding events in American history to inspire, is the basis of a union between the North and the South, such as could not have been in the old days, when each side was taunting the other. I do not say that respect begets love, but I do say that there can be no enduring attachment between individuals or States without this solid basis of respect; and therefore I predict, as the result of the war, a Union closer and stronger than before.

It did me good to see how the Confederate officers round the table responded to this sentiment, which they emphasized, not with words so much as with grasps of the hand, that meant more than words. I looked in the face of the Governor, and saw that if it were possible that a man of his years should ever again ride forth to battle, it would be to fight for the flag and the country. He beckoned me to his side, and I sat down by him, and asked him about his old commander, Stonewall Jackson, who might have been one of Cromwell's Roundheads—a man who feared God, and therefore knew no other fear. "I was near him when he

fell," said the Governor. It was the greatest loss which
could have come to the army, except that of Lee himself,
and perhaps outweighed all that had been gained at Chancellorsville. An old Catholic priest of New Orleans, to
whom was assigned the duty of preparing a memorial address, but expressed the feeling of many in saying: " When
it was decreed in the counsels of the Almighty that the
Confederacy should not succeed, *it became necessary first to
remove Stonewall Jackson.*" Nothing but a Divine decree
could reconcile them to his loss. But for him, he died as
a soldier would wish to die, in the moment of victory. His
last words were, " Let us pass over the river, and rest
under the trees." Was this a vision in his dying eyes of
some sheltered spot on a mossy bank, or under the trees before his door? or was it a glimpse of the Far-off Country,
where " the weary are at rest "? It was to the latter that
he was to depart: for then the voice ceased, and the face
took on the look of perfect peace; the heart stood still, and
his spirit indeed " passed over the river, and rested under
the trees " in the Paradise of God.

Here we had to rise from the table, as our train was
waiting for us. The Governor shook us all warmly by the
hand as he bade us good-bye, while our younger friends
" accompanied us to the ship."

As we took our places for New Orleans, I could not
but recall an evening two years since when going over
the same ground. Then I was among strangers, and as
I sat silent in the twilight, I could not if I would avoid
hearing a conversation between two gentlemen (one of
whom sat beside me, and the other opposite) who had been
officers in the war, and found a grim delight in recalling
" moving accidents by flood and field." The one who was
the chief talker had been at one time a prisoner in the
Union lines, and had made his escape, the recital of which
stirred his blood even now after the lapse of twenty years.

As the result of his military experience, he had a decided preference as to the arm of the service in which he would choose to be. "If I were to go into the army again," he said, "I would try to obtain a commission in the artillery. An officer who has a battery of his own is much more independent than one of equal rank in the infantry, where he is quite overshadowed by his regimental or brigade commander. But with a battery of six or eight guns, he has more opportunity to distinguish himself. When the war began," he continued, "the Federals had greatly the advantage in artillery. At the battle of Malvern Hill they massed their guns so that they swept away our troops every time we attempted to advance. Later in the war we learned how to reserve our fire, and to use it with effect. But while at the beginning they had the advantage of us in artillery, we had the advantage of them in cavalry. The Southerners were born on horseback (every man on a plantation had been brought up from a boy in the saddle). This made them so dashing and fearless. It was a gallant sight to see Jeb Stewart at the head of his bold riders. He was my ideal of a cavalry officer. So great was our superiority, that our men counted it *but fun* to repel an attack of the Northern troopers. But before the war was over," the speaker frankly admitted, "this was changed. The Federals became more used to the saddle; they were well mounted and well armed, and *I tell you*," he said with emphasis, "the last year or two when they attacked us, *they gave us all we wanted to do to take care of them.*" Like the brave soldier that he appeared to be, he was ready to concede the courage of his enemy. "Never was there a more gallant charge," he said, "than that they made at Fredericksburg. How firm and steady they moved up the hill! I stood on the heights and watched it all. The Irish brigade under General Meagher had almost reached our lines, when it broke under our terrible fire."

So the talk ran on in the gloaming.   I found then, as I have found everywhere at the South, that those who served in the ranks of the Confederacy, while they do not retain a feeling of bitterness over their defeat, are yet loyal to the cause for which they fought, and feel a natural pride in re-calling deeds of daring.

And what is more, they can do justice to their adversa-ries, and this softens the pain of defeat, when they recognize the fact that they have been overcome by a gallant foe. Their military pride remains untouched by the issue of the war, and the hatred of enemies gives place to a feeling of mutual respect.   They have made the discovery, which *we* too have made, that a man may have been opposed to us in the field, and yet acted with a heart as honest, and a purpose (to him) as patriotic as ours; and when he has shown the courage of his convictions by fighting for them with the most heroic devotion, he has shown great quali-ties which we can not but admire.   The recognition of this on both sides will do more than all else to bring us together.

VI.

NEW ORLEANS—THE CITY AND THE PEOPLE—CREOLE POP-
ULATION—FRENCH GAYETY—BUSINESS INTERESTS—
THE EXPOSITION—THE CHURCHES—DR. PALMER.

THE next morning we awoke to find ourselves near the sea; sea-birds were hovering in the air; we snuffed the breeze from the Gulf; and through the level and marshy plain the trunks of trees were bearded with that long, floating moss, which gives such a weird and funereal aspect to the Southern forests; and soon we came in sight of a low-lying but vast expanse of roofs, which, with the forest of masts behind them, told us that we had reached the city which stands on the banks of the Great River, and is " nigh unto the entering in of the sea."

The first sight of New Orleans is not attractive. The country around has the appearance of being submerged, and the city itself can hardly keep its head above water. It is actually below the level of the river, and the covering of earth is so thin that it is impossible to dig a cellar or even a grave. Even the dead have to be buried in brick " ovens " above ground!

But the mere flatness of a country, though it takes away one chief element of beauty—that derived from variety of surface—does not take away *all* beauty, for the barrenness of nature may be redeemed by the skill and taste of man. The coast of Holland is below the level of the sea, which is kept out by enormous dikes; but the country is made very picturesque, for the recovered bed of the ocean is made into fat meadows, with fat cattle grazing upon them; while the landscape is varied by canals and windmills and church spires, peering out from among the trees.

But New Orleans has scarcely anything which can be called picturesque. With only a flat, watery surface to stand upon, no wonder that it is spilled out and spread out in almost limitless extent. The city is laid out at right angles, and the streets are of interminable length, and some of them of a corresponding width. Canal street, which divides the old or French part of the town from the newer or American part, is a good deal wider than the Bowery, the widest of our New York streets. An avenue so broad, running through the heart of a great city, might be imposing if it were lined with palaces like those of Rome, or built up like the Boulevards of Paris. But here there is not the slightest attempt at the grand in architecture, or even at uniformity. The Custom House is about the only building that can claim to be at all imposing, while the street is largely given up to shops, some of which are quite insignificant and unworthy of such a situation. If I had been content with the first impression as I rode through it, I should have gone away with the opinion that New Orleans was only a second or third-rate American city!

But cities, like men, sometimes improve upon acquaintance, and after being a few days in New Orleans, I confess to have contracted a fondness for the old city.

First of all, it is unique among American cities. It has a character of its own: it is not like anything else. If it is not grand, it is quaint and curious and old; and this is something in a country where so many of our towns are "brand-new," huge piles of brick and boards, with the paint fresh upon them. For its unique character, it is sometimes spoken of in connection with Quebec, though the two cities are as unlike as can be; yet they agree in this: that neither is made after the regulation pattern. In walking about the old town, which is occupied chiefly by the French, one might believe himself in one of the provinces of France—in a mediæval city of Normandy or Brittany.

He would recognize the faces as French, even if he did not hear the French language. Thus New Orleans revives impressions of the old world in a very delightful way.

The French element has given a French gayety even to the American population. Nowhere this side the ocean is the Carnival observed with so much spirit. Especially on the last day, the Mardi Gras, the city runs riot with mirth and festivity. There is a King of the Carnival, who, assuming his royal title of REX, issues his sovereign decrees to "his loyal subjects" for the proper observance of the fête, on the day that he enters "his favorite city of pleasure and enjoyment!" Two years since we chanced to arrive here at the time of this season of gayety. When we heard of it we would have postponed our visit, but it was too late, and we had to be spectators, for which, however, we were not sorry, as it was a curious exhibition of fun and folly, to be seen nowhere else on this continent. As our rooms opened on a balcony which looked out upon Canal street, we could see the processions as they passed. There were several series of tableaux, chiefly representing ancient or sacred history, which showed considerable artistic skill, and could only have been got up at great expense: it was said that they cost over a hundred thousand dollars. They showed best in the evening, when seen by the light of torches and of a general illumination of the streets. Some of our party who had had opportunity to make the comparison, said they were much more effective than what they saw at the Carnival in Rome.

But to sober, work-a-day people, amusement, if too prolonged, becomes wearisome, and "cold-blooded Northerners" sometimes turn abruptly from the spectacle of the Mardi Gras to ask what New Orleans "does for a living?" They are then taken to the Cotton Exchange, for at the South it is still true that cotton is king. Its cultivation is still the great Southern industry, of which the Exchange in

New Orleans is the head-center, as here merchants and brokers meet to buy and sell, and bulletins are posted, giving the price of cotton in all the leading markets of the world. To judge from the number of persons so engaged, the interest involved must be enormous. Not only is the product vast in amount, but it is made by modern processes to yield more than ever before. The cotton-seed, which a few years since was thrown away as worthless, is now made to yield an oil which is a valuable article of commerce. After being expressed from the seed, it passes through a process of refining, from which it reappears of a beautiful clearness and color. We were told that it was exported in great quantities to France and Italy, from which it is again imported into this country as the finest olive oil! It is also used extensively here at home in the production of that manufactured butter which has of late invaded our markets, to the consternation of farmers and dairymen. Some who know more about the matter than I do, tell me that this is a very harmless compound, the chief ingredient of which is lard. Now I know there is nothing in lard which is "common or unclean," *when used in the right place.* Did not our mothers use it to make the delicious, flakey crust of the mince-pies which graced our tables on Thanksgiving-day? But somehow it seems as if the very same article would not taste quite the same if made into butter. But I am told that I "can not tell the difference." Indeed a very dear friend of mine tells me that he "can beat any cow in the world;" that his butter is never rancid; and that he is always sure of having it of that fine flavor and that rich yellow color which are so much prized in the products of the dairy. Still I reject all his arguments as temptations of the adversary, and protest that, rather than be thus deceived, I will have my little Jersey cows driven up to my door (as they do with the goats in France), and milked before my eyes, and will keep a watch on the churning. In this way I trust I shall be able to spread my bread with good, honest, old-fashioned butter to the end of my days.

Speaking of Southern industries reminds us of the Exposition, which was so brilliant last year, and the ghost of which still survives, though its glory is departed. A friend drove me out to the grounds, which are several miles from the city. The buildings were still standing, and the Exposition still nominally open, though it was but the shadow of its former self, as the rich exhibits of foreign countries had been removed, and little remained except the natural and manufactured products of our own country, and these in diminished form; so that the vast range of buildings was " a banquet-hall deserted." Yet the Exposition of last year was one of the most notable that this country has ever seen. It is said that it was not a financial success. That may be: and yet many things which are not successful as a mere speculation, are greatly to the advantage of the public. And this certainly was an immense benefit to New Orleans and the South. The tens of thousands of visitors whom it brought here, added millions to the income of the Crescent City. Still greater was the gain to the Southern States in the display it made of their products, such as had never been seen before. Considering all this, I think they owe a debt of gratitude to the distinguished Editor, Major E. A. Burke, of "The Times-Democrat," by whose energy this great result was achieved. To him more than to any other man it is due that the world now understands how vast are the resources of the South, and the materials of its wealth and power.

From the Exposition to the river is four miles, and as the road was in fine condition, and as my friend had a beautiful pair of horses, we went spinning over it, not exactly at a Presbyterian gait, but with a speed that made my blood tingle. Arrived at the Mississippi, we climbed the dikes made to protect the country from inundation, and found that since our former visit a second embankment had been added to keep the river in bounds. It is a terrible destroyer, against which it is necessary to keep watch night and day at the time of the annual floods. This system of levees extends along the Mississippi for hundreds of miles. It must cost a heavy sum to the city and the State to keep them in repair, though nothing as yet to compare with the expenditure of Holland, where one third the revenues of the State is applied to keep out the waves of the German Ocean. It has often been proposed that the " walling-in " of the Mississippi be undertaken by the Government as a national work, and very elaborate plans have been made by engineers, the cost of which, it is estimated, would be over thirty millions; but it would reclaim and keep for perpetual cultivation a body of land equal in extent (at least so I judge merely from the eye), as well as in richness, to the Valley of the Nile from Cairo to the First Cataract.

After so much to fill the eye and the mind, it is pleasant to have one day intervene before we enter on more sight-seeing. To no one is the day of rest more welcome than to the weary traveller. There is something in the very atmosphere that is soothing and restful. The city has put on its " Sunday's best." All whom you meet walk slowly, and not with the hurried step of other days. Their blood seems to flow more quietly in their veins. The air, unvexed by sounds of traffic, is still, and it seems as if the sun looked out with more cheering light and warmth from the unclouded sky.

New Orleans has not the reputation of being a Sabbath-keeping city. That part of its population which is French has the national preference for an European Sunday rather than an American Sabbath. But still there is (if I may judge from my observation, which is of course very limited),

even among the Creoles, a respect for the day such as I
have not seen in France. To be sure, in the morning the
markets are open, and there is the usual chaffering and
jabbering; but an hour or two later the Creole dames, in
their white caps, may be seen flocking to the numerous
Catholic churches for mass. In the afternoon they ride
out with their husbands and children to some public garden
on the banks of the Mississippi, and in the evening the
theatres are open. Thus the day is kept as a holiday rather
than as a holy day. But at least it is not so much profaned by hard, grinding labor. I saw no house-building
going on, as one sees in Paris. To this extent at least it is
a day of physical rest.

But if half the city is Catholic, there is another portion
which is stoutly Protestant, and as rigidly observant of the
Lord's-day as the people of New York or New England.
In the morning I met Mr. Sankey in the breakfast-room at
the St. Charles, which reminded me that Mr. Moody was
now holding a series of meetings here, one of which I at-
tended in the evening.

But apart from the gatherings drawn by such special
services, there is in New Orleans a Christian community,
composed of churches of different denominations, which is
a powerful element in the city. The pastor of the Presbyterian church in Lafayette Square, Dr. B. M. Palmer, is
perhaps the man of most power and influence to be found
in any denomination in the South. It was a great pleasure
to listen to such a prince of preachers, whose ideas are not
chaotic, like those of many of the brilliant " pulpit ora-
tors " of the day, but who has in his mind a clear, well-
defined system of truth, which he firmly believes. His
mind is logical; it moves, not in an eccentric orbit, but in
a straight line, advancing from one position to another. It
is an intellectual study to observe his way of opening a subject: how he accumulates proof upon proof, and argument

upon argument, marshalling them one after the other with a military precision. Thus he moves upon the enemy's works, not in a skirmish line, but in ranks and battalions, sweeping everything before him. Nor does he stop with intellectual conviction, but enforces the truth with the most direct personal application. Old Lyman Beecher used to define eloquence as "logic on fire"—a phrase which describes exactly that of Dr. Palmer. It is refreshing in these days of puny preachers, who hesitate and stammer even over the words of the Almighty, to listen to one who knows what he believes, and whose force of conviction speaks out in his clear, ringing voice. Such faith in the preacher inspires faith in the hearers, and thus it is that men are built up and established in the truth.

Very different was the scene at night, when three thousand people gathered in the largest hall of the city to hear Mr. Moody, whose style is the greatest possible contrast to that of Dr. Palmer, as he seems, in his free, off-hand way, to disdain logic, and yet he has a logic of his own; though he is so eager to get close to his hearers that he is impatient at being delayed by formal arguments. If we might compare him to a soldier, we should say that he was so fierce to be at the enemy that he leaped over the breastworks to come to close quarters. To-night he spoke from the parable of the guests invited to the supper, all of whom "began to make excuse." He enumerated these excuses, and as he held them up one after another, he literally tore them to pieces with fiery indignation. I never heard him speak with so much power before. Mr. Sankey sung

"Jesus of Nazareth passeth by,"

which recalled the sweet Sabbath evening that I heard it in Nazareth itself; and

"When the clouds have rolled away,"

a song which pierces the heart like an arrow, causing us at
the same moment to weep and to rejoice, as we think of
the manifold griefs and anxieties which hang darkly over
this life, and of the time when all these " clouds " shall be
swept from the heaven, and we shall see only our Father's
face. The meeting was followed by one of inquiry, hundreds moving toward the room in rear of the hall to listen
to Mr. Moody's more direct personal appeals.

Shall I be told that I let my thoughts wander in bye-
and forbidden-places, if I confess that I enjoyed the services of this day the more because of the consciousness that,
though far away from home, I was still in " my own, my
native land " ? Had the Southern Confederacy been established by war, I should now be in a foreign country, and
even the prayers of the house of God would not have been
to me the same, and the dear old familiar hymns would not
have fallen on the ear so sweetly as they do now. I should
have said in my heart, like the Jews in Babylon, " How can
I sing the Lord's song in a strange land?" No; that was
not to be. Had it been, we of the North should not be
here to-day. We could not walk these streets feeling that
we were " aliens from the commonwealth " of this portion
of our American Israel.

VII.

EXCURSION ACROSS THE MISSISSIPPI—OLD ESTATES IN NEW
HANDS—THE SALT MINES AT AVERY'S ISLAND—THE
BAYOU TÊCHE AND THE ACADIANS.

AMONG other excursions planned for our entertainment
by our friends, who are always looking out for something
pleasant for us, was an excursion across the river, to visit
some remarkable salt mines at a trifling distance of a hundred and forty miles or so. I had been over the route before, on my way to Southern California, but was glad to go
again. Being of a somewhat impressible nature, I can not
help getting into a fit of musing in crossing a great river.
The Mississippi is to me more imposing than the Nile,
though it have not its hoary antiquity, nor be invested with
the mystery which for so many ages surrounded the source
of the great river of Africa. But it seems to me to have
more breadth and depth, a greater volume and *power of
destruction*. I look at it with a feeling of awe as it sweeps
on its mighty flood, telling as it goes the story of the far-off
latitude in which it had its birth, and of the rains and
snows on distant mountains by which it has been swollen
till it has accumulated a power which nothing can resist.
Nor is it without a history. It was in 1541—nearly eighty
years before the Pilgrim Fathers landed on Plymouth Rock
—that De Soto discovered the Great River, only to die on
its banks, and be buried in its waters. For nearly three
centuries and a half it has rolled over the bones of its dis-
coverer, its placid surface unvexed by all the woes and agi-
tations of this troubled world. Is there in nature, unless
it be in the sea itself, a grander symbol of the government

of God, sweeping on through the ages, unchecked by the power or the violence of man?

But here we are on the other side of the river. We have a long ride before us, but one does not count distances with good company. Mr. Hutchinson (the courteous manager of the Southern Pacific Railroad, who was himself detained by a strike on the freight lines) gave us as a substitute his faithful lieutenant, Mr. Randolph Natili, whose name bespeaks his Italian parentage, but who has also French and Greek blood in his veins: so that he is one of those cosmopolites, knowing half a dozen languages and at home in any country, whom Cook of London picks up wherever he can find them, to be the guides of his travelling parties on the Continent and in the East. A more agreeable cicerone never took charge of a party. As he had been for years connected with the road, he knew every step of the way, and gave us the history of the country through which we passed, the names of the places and the character of the people.

The country itself is not picturesque. It is a sort of amphibious region, like one of its own crocodiles, with its head on dry land, while the rest of the slimy creature is submerged in water. One fifth of the State of Louisiana is subject to inundations, though not every year. Those who have seen the salt marshes in Holland, or on the coast of England, have the exact counterpart of the Delta of the Mississippi, which has been formed by the soil thrown up by the river as it pushes its way into the waters of the Gulf. It was all once lying at the bottom of the sea, from which it has emerged in the slow lapse of ages. Indeed, it has not its head fully out of water yet, and seems to linger like a shy nymph of the sea-caves, reluctant to leave her watery home. And yet even this half-risen condition has a beauty of its own in this very mingling of land and water, as low spits of earth run out into the sea, and long bayous

stretch upward like the lagoons of Venice, till sea and land
are locked together by their mutually embracing arms.
True, such a vast reach of low-lying country is monotonous,
yet there is a certain grandeur even in monotony when it
stretches on into infinity.   In a few weeks the country will
take on a marvellous richness of color, as the trees put forth
their leaves, the wild flowers bloom, and the whole land is
covered with a semi-tropical vegetation.

As might be expected from the alluvial character of the
soil, it is of boundless fertility.   We are now in the region
of sugar plantations; and the negroes are abroad in the
cane-fields, which are of vast extent.   Some are plowing,
turning up the rich black earth to be warmed by the sun
(for, although it is but the 15th of February, the Spring-
time has come); while others, men and women, are bring-
ing out the cane.   All have an air of comfort and content.
"They hear not the task-master's voice."   It is a source
of endless delight to me to look into their happy faces.   If
we had a miserable pessimist on board, who thinks every-
thing going to "the everlasting bow-wows," I would put
him at one of our windows, where he could catch a glimpse
of those rows of shining teeth, as the creatures laugh from
ear to ear.   I shouldn't wonder if that tall chap yonder
called himself Abraham Lincoln, for his legs are about as
long as "Old Abe's."   But Lincoln never had such a feeling of pride as his black namesake when he mounts to ride
across the fields to his little cabin for dinner.   A darkey
on a mule is at a height of earthly grandeur in which he
does not feel himself to be inferior to Alexander or Napoleon.   Care sits on him as loosely as his ragged pantaloons,
and if anything should trouble him for a moment, he kicks
it off as he would an old shoe.

We were greatly amused with the pickaninnies, that were
lying about the cabins, like so many Indian papooses, roast-
ing their woolly heads in the sun.   Once indeed we tried to

cultivate their acquaintance, though with a result not altogether satisfactory. We had stopped at a station to take
in water, when Mr. Inman and I walked toward a cabin a
few rods away, on the porch of which sat a colored woman
with two children, one of whom was choking himself with
cabbage that he was stuffing into his mouth. We wanted
to ask how she and her people were getting along. But
she was suspicious of white folks, and started up like a bear
that is about to be robbed of her whelps. She seized the
cubs as if she thought they were going to be stolen by a
slave-trader, and started away, muttering savagely, "We
has to be keerful what kind o' folks comes round now'days."
We did not presume to make any further advance, but as we
turned on our heels, heard her hissing between her teeth
that "she didn't want nothing to do with no sich kind o'
white folks!" This was the first snub that we had received in
all the South. Our fellow-travellers laughed heartily, telling us "we had caught a Tartar," and set her down as
"an ill-tempered wench." But for my part, I pitied the
poor woman, thinking that she may have received rudeness
from some strangers, which made her suspicious of all.
By and by she will be subdued by gentleness and patience.
I never saw any human creature so wild that could not be
tamed by kindness.

But while the lot of the negroes in Louisiana has been
lightened, that of their old masters has darkened. The
abolition of slavery made a total change in the condition of
the Southern planters. In the old days they lived in an
easy sort of way—always in debt, to be sure; always pledg-
ing their sugar and cotton in advance; but still they had
the land and the negroes to work it, and so they managed
to make the two ends meet, and kept things going from
year to year. But when at a single blow they were stripped
of their labor, they had not the capacity nor the training to
teach them how to adapt themselves to their changed con-

dition; it was hard to economize; it was much easier to
borrow; and so they went on until almost every plantation
was mortgaged to creditors in New Orleans, and sunk
deeper and deeper under debt, till at last it was swallowed
up in the abyss. As we passed a plantation, Natili, who
knows all the great estates, pointed us to a famous old
mansion, connected with which was a pitiful story. It had
been in the family for generations, and been the scene of
boundless festivity and hospitality; but the estate had been
gradually sinking in the general ruin, until a few weeks
since the owner, a lady ninety-four years of age, who had
been a Grandissime indeed, left her old home, where she
had spent her life in affluence and luxury, and moved into
the house of her overseer, there to end her days! Could
anything be more pathetic than this—an aged woman, having a rich inheritance and a proud name, compelled at last
to leave the family mansion, and take refuge under the roof
of one of her former dependents, where she finds shelter
only to die—too happy when death closes her eyes on the
scene of her former pride and present humiliation!

It was two o'clock when we drew up at New Iberia, and,
deflecting our course from the trunk line, which keeps
steadily toward the setting sun till it touches the Pacific,
we darted off nine miles to Avery's Island, which, by the
way, is *not* an island, but a peninsula—a promontory pro-
jecting into the Gulf, but still linked by a narrow neck with
the land. These "islands" are a feature of this coast,
and are often extremely beautiful. On an adjoining one
Joe Jefferson, the actor, spends a portion of each year (he
is there now: his son went down in the mine with us), enjoying the restful solitude, and drinking in health from
the air of the sea.

Here was discovered a little more than twenty years ago
the most remarkable deposit of salt to be found in the country. I do not wonder that the Southern people looked

upon its discovery as Providential: for it came during the war, at a time when the Confederacy was hard pressed for salt, as it was for many other things, when every spring in the mountains which had even a slight saline mixture, was carefully sought out, and the water evaporated to furnish what is almost a necessary of life. But here was a *mine*, where the rock-salt lay not only in beautiful crystals, but in great masses, to be quarried like blocks of granite. The more it was explored, the richer it proved. Descending a shaft more than a hundred feet in depth, we found ourselves in a vast cavern, like one of the numerous chambers in the Mammoth Cave of Kentucky, or the Grotto of Adelsberg in Austria. From the center, side-chambers branch off in every direction. The effect was very striking as the blue lights that were burned at a distance were reflected from the sides around and the arches above. It was as weird a scene as one could imagine in some vaulted chamber of the under-world. The salt is mined like coal, the solid walls being drilled with holes, and blasted away with dynamite or giant-powder. These blocks, after being broken into portable size, are carried up the shaft, and ground to fine powder for table-salt. The amount sent abroad is immense. Mr. Armour found here three of his Refrigerator cars waiting to be loaded for their great cattle-yards in Kansas City. The Armour Brothers of Chicago pay nearly a million of dollars a year for salt alone!

After this most interesting subterranean visit, we came to the light of day, and walked perhaps a mile to the house of the Averys, who are the owners of the island and the mine. The house stands on a knoll which commands as pretty a view as one could wish to behold. Where could one look out on a more delightful combination of land and sea than sitting on this broad veranda, turning on one side to the vast lowlands backed by great forests; and on the other to the watery plain, broken only by the white caps of waves, and the sails of ships passing along the horizon?

In harmony with so much beauty without, was the interior of this old mansion, where, though strangers, we were entertained with the kindest hospitality. It was pleasant to find on this Southern verge of the Republic those who were linked by many ties with the North, where they had friends and relatives, and were educating children in Northern schools and colleges. Mr. Hall found that they had kindred in his father's church in New York. Among the memories of our journey to the South, none is more pleasant than that of the visit to Avery's Island.

When we came back to New Iberia, I begged my friends to hold up a little till I could take a quick walk through the village, and over the bridge which spans the famous Bayou Têche, the scene of the closing part of Longfellow's "Evangeline"—a country which Mr. Charles A. Dana had excited my desire to see by the description which he gave me of a visit several years since with Lieutenant-Governor Dorsheimer. They went up the bayou in a steam-launch, and could take in all the beauties of stream and forest. I could only come to the water-side, and as I stood on the bridge, look longingly up and down the stream. The beauty of scenery, I am sure, is not overdrawn, and I can well believe that the legend of "Evangeline" is founded on a true story. But though the country is still occupied by the simple Acadians, whose ancestors came hither from Nova Scotia at the beginning of the last century, they do not seem to me a very interesting people. Though of French descent, they are quite different from the Creoles of New Orleans, and speak a different patois. Their lives are circumscribed within a very narrow circle, their chief excitement being the numerous feasts and saints' days. They are literally "islanded" in these bayous, where they are shut out from the world almost as much as if they were in the island of Juan Fernandez with Robinson Crusoe.

The only influence which can penetrate these sylvan shades is the omnipresent Newspaper, and how it may find its way here I learned from Major Burke of "The Times-Democrat," to whom New Orleans is indebted for its Great Exhibition. He had taken Mr. Dana and Mr. Dorsheimer up the Bayou in his private launch, which he told me he had built for a business purpose, viz: to run up all these bayous to canvass for his paper. He put aboard of it half a dozen of his brightest reporters, and mounted a cannon on the forward deck. As soon as it came in sight of a village it banged away, which woke up the sleepy *habitans*, who rushed down to the landing to see what was the matter, while the daughters of the village came flocking behind. These were welcomed on board, and maidens and reporters were soon whirling in a dance. After this "the boys" gave marvellous descriptions of the village, as the most delicious retreat in the shadow of "the forest primeval," a spot too sweet and pure to be profaned by the feet of common men; but which was occupied by a simple pastoral race, whose virtues were in harmony with the natural beauty of the scenes amid which they dwelt. Of course this "brought down" the simple-minded Acadians, and the thrifty proprietor raked in a large addition to the subscribers to his paper, which soon attained an immense circulation! This was a degree of enterprise which the most ingenious Yankee could not equal. I wonder that the Salvation Army has not hit upon the same device, and that it does not now and then rig up a steam launch to penetrate these hidden bayous, and have it mounted with a Gospel gun, that should stir the echoes of the forest, and almost wake the dead!

When we took our places in the car, we were homeward

bound.   The sun was setting behind us, casting his last
rays over the broad landscape, and soon the twilight came
on; but as we sat in the gloaming, the incidents of the day
gave a pleasant turn to our thoughts.   We stopped but
once, to leave our friend Natili at his home in Morgan
City, forty miles from New Orleans, and an hour later saw
the lights of the great city reflected in the waters of the
great river.

VIII

MEMORIES OF THE LOST CAUSE—SOUTHERN LEADERS—
CONVERSATION WITH GENERAL BEAUREGARD ABOUT
BULL RUN—ALBERT SIDNEY JOHNSTON, JEFFERSON
DAVIS, AND GENERAL LEE.

WHEN I came to New Orleans two years since, Senator
Gibson, of Louisiana, gave me a letter to General Beauregard, who did me the honor to call upon me. As he entered the room I observed, as I thought, a resemblance to another illustrious Frenchman whom I had met in Cairo two years before—M. de Lesseps. I speak of General Beauregard as a Frenchman; for, though a native of New Orleans, as were his father and grandfather before him, yet his father was born here when Louisiana belonged to France, and continued to live here when it was ceded to Spain, and when still later it was ceded to the United States; so that, while living in one and the same city, he had lived under three governments requiring three allegiances. In such changes one could hardly expect a very pronounced loyalty from father or son. General Beauregard told me that he could not speak English till he was twelve years old. That in a civil war he should cast in his lot with the people of his own State, whose language he spoke, is less surprising than the contrary would have been.

It was a new experience to find myself face to face with the man who had fired on Fort Sumter, and who had won the first battle of the war. As I led the way to these eventful periods of his career, of course not to provoke controversy, but to draw him out, he spoke of them not boastfully, but freely. I was especially interested to hear details of the Battle of Bull Run. It was a curious coincidence that the two commanders in that battle, Beauregard and McDowell, had been classmates at West Point, and that having been students in the art of war, in the same military school, under the same teachers, they were now to be pitted against each other in the field. To my remark that military authorities had said that McDowell's dispositions for the battle were excellent, but were defeated by those unexpected and inexplicable complications which often defeat the best plans in war, he answered that " his fatal mistake was in not attacking in force the first day;" that he was then greatly superior in numbers, and that if he had attacked then, he (McDowell) would have *smashed* him! But the delay of two or three days gave time to bring ten thousand men from Richmond, and other re-enforcements from the army of Joseph E. Johnston, so that he was able to take the offensive.

He described very vividly the crisis of the battle, when the latter force was coming on the ground. He saw a movement in the distance of troops approaching, but could not at first tell whether they were friends or foes. The flag then used by the Confederates differed but little from that of the Union; it was not easy to distinguish the stars and bars from the stars and stripes. It was a hot day in July, and the flag hung by the staff. For a few minutes he was in intense anxiety. At length a light breeze caused the drooping ensign to unroll, and as it was flung out by the wind he recognized the flag of the Confederacy, and instantly despatched his officers in every direction to order a general advance, and the day was won.

" But," I ventured to ask, " if General McDowell made a fatal error in not attacking before your re-enforcements came up, did you not make a similar mistake in not pressing your advantages after the battle? Why did you not march upon Washington while our troops were demoralized by defeat? In the panic you might have taken the capital, and perhaps ended the war."

No doubt he had often heard this suggestion before, to which he was prepared with a reply. He thought it would not have been so easy, even at that moment, to capture Washington; for that even a small force, by planting cannon so as to sweep the Long Bridge, could have prevented his crossing; while, he said, vessels of war were lying in the Potomac, with heavy guns, which, moving up and down the river, could sweep its banks. But he added that a week or two after he thought he *could* have taken the city by marching his army higher up to a point where he could ford the Potomac. Had I asked him why he did not, I presume he would answer that he was overruled by Mr. Davis, who was disposed to be very cautious, and not to peril the advantage already gained by any rash movement. He might have used still stronger language: for there is no love lost between him and the late President of the Confederacy, whom he regards as his evil genius, defeating his best-laid plans, and so preventing the other and greater victories which he would have won.

In repeating this conversation I violate no confidence, for General Beauregard only gave me in brief what he has stated at far greater length in his published volumes. But there was a peculiar interest in hearing these details of that first battle from the lips of the chief actor in it. Often as we recur to that crisis of the war, we see on how slight a thing may turn momentous issues. Some may call it accident; others will call it Providence. A devout mind will recognize in small things as well as in great the hand of the supreme Disposer of events. "Man proposes, but God disposes." To us of the North that first defeat was a bitter humiliation; and yet before the war was ended we saw—or thought we saw—in it a purpose of wisdom and of goodness. Had we been victorious in that first battle the

movement of secession might have been crushed in its very
beginning, and the Union restored without those long years
of battle and blood, of mourning and woe.   Yet at what a
price should we have bought a peace—at the price of con-
cessions in which the North would have sacrificed all its
principles, and slavery would have been made stronger
than ever, to be preserved and perpetuated for generations
to come.   This was not to be.   The Ruler of nations had
His own ends to accomplish.   To that end was needed a
people in another temper than that of compromise.   It
needed that first defeat, that stinging lesson, to arouse the
North, and nerve it to a four years' struggle.   So God led
us on, not by the way of uniform success, over the heights
of victory, but often through the deep valley of humiliation, to bring us to the great deliverance which He had in
reserve for us—that of a restored country and of universal
liberty.

But the Battle of Bull Run was not the only instance in
the war in which the fate of the country seemed to hang
on a thread.   Another instance was brought to my attention in New Orleans in conversing with another gentleman, who, if not so prominent an actor in those scenes as
General Beauregard, was a most intelligent spectator of
them—a man of New England ancestry and education,
whose grandparents were on one side from Massachusetts,
and on the other from Connecticut, and who is himself a
graduate of Yale.   I refer to Col. Preston Johnston, one
of the most cultivated men in the South.   He is a son of
Gen. Albert Sidney Johnston, who commanded the Confederate army at the Battle of Shiloh (or Pittsburg Landing), whose Life he has written, in preparing for which he
has of course collected with the utmost care the details of
the battle in which his father fell; and he gave me his decided opinion (an opinion shared, I am told, by the great
body of Confederate officers who took part in the battle)

that " when he was shot and fell from his horse *he had gained a great victory ;* and that if he had not been killed at that critical moment, in two hours more *he would have captured Gen. Grant and his whole army !*" Of course this opinion is stoutly disputed by writers on our side, yet I believe even they admit that the Union forces were strained to the very last point to hold their ground until the arrival of Gen. Buell; and it is at least possible that the continued assault of the Confederate army under the same commander, who had been so brilliantly successful in the earlier part of the day, *might* have made the success complete! If so, here is one more illustration of the truth so often taught in history, that issues of the highest moment may turn on the life or death of one man!

Few men have had a better opportunity to know the inside history of the war than Col. Johnston, as he was on the staff of Jefferson Davis, and in a position to observe the intrigues and rivalries and ambitions of leaders in the army and in Confederate politics. I was curious to know how Mr. Davis was regarded by one who had been in his intimacy; whether he was one of the men who appear great at a distance, and grow small as they are approached; but lest the question should be embarrassing, I put it in a guarded way, which admitted of a vague and general answer, that would not commit him who gave it. But he answered without the least reserve, and while he might have been influenced by a feeling of loyalty to his chief, yet he spoke with the utmost candor and sincerity. He said Mr. Davis always impressed him as a truly great man; and as to his integrity, he was so inflexibly honest—he had so little of the spirit of a demagogue—that he lost popularity by refusing to stoop to the common arts for conciliating opposition. Where ordinary politicians would have used money from the Secret Service Fund to bribe the press, or have distributed military titles, which he had in his gift, to secure the support of men who were lukewarm or hostile, he absolutely refused to expend a dollar, or to give a single commission, which was not strictly in the line of his public duty.

This was a new view of the "arch-rebel," but one which I was glad to receive; for I do not like to think of any man who is evil spoken of, that he is as black as he is painted. Nor have I any reason to doubt the correctness of the portrait here drawn. John C. Calhoun, the life-long defender of Slavery, was a man of stainless character, who acted from a high sense of honor and of duty. Of course that did not make his political theories the less dangerous. Such cases rather prove that a false principle carried out with inexorable logic, may be as destructive to the peace of a State and the happiness of a people as the most selfish ambition.

But the name which evokes most popular enthusiasm at the South, is not that of Jefferson Davis, but of Gen. Lee, of which New Orleans furnished a striking proof two years since on the unveiling of a statue in bronze of the Confederate Chief, which had been erected in one of the public squares. The work had been in progress for some time; for the statue surmounts a lofty column, or obelisk, apparently designed to suggest a resemblance to the Column of Napoleon in the Place Vendome in Paris. The statue is not a great work of art. The figure is rather heavy, not to say clumsy. Of course it had to be of colossal size, to be in proportion at such a height. The great soldier has no sign of his rank, wearing only his sword and belt. He has not even a military cap on his head, but the soft felt hat which his soldiers knew so well. Still there is something majestic in that martial figure, with arms folded as if in meditation, standing aloft against the sky.

The statue was unveiled on the 22d of February, the birthday of Washington. The occasion brought together a concourse which filled the whole square, and overflowed into the adjoining streets. In the military procession Union soldiers took part as well as Confederates. One who was " a looker-on " told me that it was very touching to observe the contrast between the blue coats and the gray, the Northern soldiers coming on the ground in fresh uniforms, with arms glistening and bands playing; while the Confederates showed but too well that the war had left them little to expend on the mere trappings of a military parade. But these old soldiers had no reason to be ashamed of garments which they had worn through successive campaigns. As they gathered round the base of the column, and looked upward, their breasts swelled with pride and their eyes filled with tears, as if they were under the eye of one whom they had so often followed through the smoke of battle.

But while the hour was full of stirring memories, there were no unseemly boastings, no bitter words or harsh recriminations, to mar the tender character of a scene which was not a revival of the spirit of war, but rather a Festival of Peace, since in it those who had once been enemies— soldiers of the North and of the South—joined to pay a tribute to one whom history will recognize as at least a great Commander.

But mere military genius, however great, can not explain the sentiment which one finds in all the South for the memory of Gen. Lee. There must have been something in the man, as well as in the soldier, to kindle such enthusiasm. What was it that inspired such a feeling in the breasts of a whole people? Few had a better opportunity to know him than Col. Johnston, who as a Professor in the College at Lexington, Va., was associated with him for four years. To him Robert E. Lee was the ideal of manhood. His very form and bearing, like those of Washington, united grace with dignity. " I never saw him," he said, " sit or stand in an ungraceful attitude. I never heard him say a word which I would rather had not been spoken—never a word in the humblest presence which might not have been said in any presence. And this not because he was on his guard, studying his words, but because his nature was simple and pure, noble and good. The impression of greatness which one had who saw him in the field, was not spoiled by any littleness in his more quiet hours. In private intercourse he was so gentle and so considerate of others, that he won the hearts of all around him, and those who knew him best loved him most."

This tenderness for others wore upon him after the war perhaps more than the fatigues of his campaigns. Nor did he find relief in venting his indignation upon his enemies. Some Southerners, like Toombs of Georgia, found comfort in cursing the North. It " did them good " to let off their violence and rage. Old Jubal Early, who has the reputation of being very profane, has been heard to say " If Gen. Lee had only taken it out now and then, as I do, in a good swear, he would be alive at this day!" But Gen. Lee was made of other stuff. He could not " take it out " in cursing. That would not drown the cry of those who wept for the dead, and had no comforter. Reflection on all the sorrow that he witnessed, clouded the evening of his days, and hastened his end. Col. Johnston, who watched with him a few nights before he breathed his last, tells me that though some temporary cause may have brought on the last illness, it was the opinion of the physicians that the real cause of death lay further back—that *he died of a broken heart!* None who saw him in those last years doubted that he suffered keenly—not for himself, for the failure of his military plans, or the defeat of his ambition, but at all the misery which had come upon the people whom he loved. He saw the South ruined by the war—its once happy homes made desolate, sons and brothers lying on a hundred battle-fields, while mothers and daughters and sisters were reduced to utter penury. From all that broad territory came up the wail of widows and orphans, and the cry entered into his ear and into his soul. This "burst his mighty heart," and he laid him down among the mountains of his beloved Virginia, and died almost without speaking a word!

Such a death was the fitting end of such a life, and intensified the feeling with which the people of the South regarded their chieftain. To them he was greater in defeat than he would have been even in victory. He not only led them to many triumphs, but when disaster came he drank with them the bitter cup; he shared their sorrows, and in his sympathy with his stricken people, showed that great as he was as a soldier, he was still greater as a man.

All this came to my mind as I stood at the foot of that column just at evening, and looked up at that bronze figure as it caught the last rays of the setting sun. If the spirits of the dead come back to visit familiar scenes, may not that of the great Commander sometimes hover about this column, not as the monument of his glory, but from that height to look abroad upon the land which was so dear to him when living? If there be sadness in his eye, as he remembers all its sorrows, may it not light up with a gleam of brightness at its returning prosperity?

The war is ended, but its fruits remain—fruits not of bitterness, but of blessing, of a better mutual understanding and increased mutual respect. I believe that the South is to have a future far greater than her past. With universal liberty has already come a new element of life, the forerunner of a progress such as she has never known before. If this continues, in another generation all the brightness of her former history will be cast far into shadow by her coming glory.

4

IX.

THE LAST HOSPITALITY—A DINNER WITH CONFEDERATE OFFICERS — HOW NORTHERN AND SOUTHERN MEN CAN TALK ABOUT THE WAR.

It was our last night in New Orleans, and our kind friends would not let us depart without one more experience of Southern hospitality. Colonel A. H. May had invited us to meet a number of gentlemen of the city at dinner. Looking round the long table, I inquired of one at my side the names of the guests, and learned that every Southern man had been a Confederate officer. With them was seated Major Throckmorton of the United States Army, now on duty in New Orleans.

After we had partaken of the generous repast, Colonel May rose and gave a hearty welcome to his Northern guests, referring to them individually as men distinguished in the commercial world, to whom he and his friends were glad tô do honor. Others spoke in the same cordial manner. Across the table from me sat a brother-in-law of General Dick Taylor, who, like that famous commander, was one of the fighting men of the war. When General Banks went up the Red River on his disastrous expedition, this gentleman, then a young officer, got a few rusty cannon and blazed away at our gunboats, which was thought at the time to be a very daring exploit. To-night he spoke in a hearty, manly way, like the brave soldier that he is— a mode of "assault" that is the most sure to be followed by "unconditional surrender."

After so many kind words, there must needs be some reply, and my fellow-travellers seemed to think that that

friendly office belonged to me. Of course the interest of
what is said on such an occasion is only for the moment.
Nor do I attach the slightest importance to it *except for the
way in which it was received*. As such, it may have some
value as showing the feeling of the South toward the North
since the war. Seeing how kindly it was taken, I have
tried to think what it was that called forth such a warm
response. The remarks were quite informal, and it is impossible to recall them precisely. And yet the occasion is
so distinctly in mind, as is my own feeling at being in a
group of Confederate officers, that I think I can give an
outline of what I said. As near as I can remember, it
was in substance as follows:

"It is very kind of you, Sir, and of the distinguished
company which you have gathered round this table, to receive us in this way. We come among you as strangers,
and you make us feel that we are no longer strangers, but
friends. You throw open your doors to us: we sit at your
table; we eat of your bread and drink of your cup; and
thus are treated as if we were part of the family, members
of your own household. There must be something in your
Southern climate that warms the blood and the heart. For
some days past we have felt that we were breathing a new
atmosphere: it was not that we had left behind our cold
Northern skies and wintry snows, and come into a region
of Spring; but (better than this) that we looked into faces
that not long ago were turned away from us, but in which
there now gleamed a returning affection, like that of
alienated brothers, who, after a separation of years, meet
under the old roof, round the old hearth-stone; and we felt
a strange thrill running along our veins as we grasped the
outstretched hand and heard the welcoming voice. These
are things which come not from any political causes, which
can not be enacted by law, nor enforced by military power.
As we sit here to-night, we are drawn to each other, not by

the force of law, but by that unwritten law of kindness,
which is the strongest tie that binds human hearts together.

"And now, Sir, will you feel that I trespass on the
courtesies of this occasion, if I speak frankly of what is in
all our hearts? There was a time when Northern men
coming South were cautioned to be very guarded in their
conversation. They might talk of the cotton crop, the
delicious climate and the peculiar vegetation of your forests,
the trees bearded with moss, and all that; but make no
allusion to ' the late unpleasantness.' This is a kind of
hypocrisy which deceives neither one side nor the other.
Why should we not talk about what we are all thinking
about, and what indeed is the greatest event in our country's history? Has not the time come when we can talk of
these things without awakening a feeling of bitterness? I
believe that where there is a right spirit (as there is getting
to be now), nothing is so helpful to mutual good-will as
absolute frankness; that the more we talk of the war—
kindly of course, but freely—the more we shall understand
each other, respect each other, and in the end love each other.

"Believing this, I venture to say a few words. Do not
be shocked if I express the opinion that the late war, terrible as it was, was yet the instrument in the hands of God
of what could be accomplished in no other way, and thus
in its issues was an immeasurable blessing both to North
and South, and as General Grant always affirmed, ' more
to the South than to the North.' Of course no minister of
religion will ever defend war as war. In itself it is one of
the greatest calamities that can come upon the human race
—a calamity with which God scourges the nations when He
would destroy them and grind them to powder. We can
not even think without horror of that terrible explosion of
human passion, in which men seem to be transformed into
wild beasts, destroying one another.

"But for all this, there are things worse than war.

National dishonor is worse; national degradation is worse.
There are times when a nation dies morally because of its
very peace and prosperity: when a people become enervated
by luxury, and sunk in universal selfishness—a hot and
stifling atmosphere, which only the fiercest thunder-storm
can drive away.   In these great struggles, while there is a
terrific display of human passion, there come out also the
noblest qualities which dignify our nature—honor, courage,
and self-sacrifice.   Thus it is that the most splendid specimens of American manhood are those which stand out
against the dark background of war.   I need not mention
names.   Southern hearts as well as Northern hearts are
full of heroic memories, which I think neither you nor we
shall be base enough to let die.

"I have heard it said that it is better to *forget* these
things.   Forget them?   Forget the greatest chapter in our
history   the greatest exhibition ever given of American
power?   True, it was a Civil War, but it was a war of
giants—a war which demonstrated as never before the
strength of the American people.   European soldiers and
statesmen looked on in wonder at the mighty struggle,
and taking it as the measure of our resources, reasoned
within themselves, If a nation can maintain such a war for
four years, and keep *two* such armies in the field, what
must be its power when these antagonists are reconciled,
and their forces are combined!

"The one great social and political result of the war
was the removal of slavery, and whether that has been a
loss or a gain, it is for you to say.   The gentleman here at
my side (a Confederate officer) tells me that it has been
an immeasurable gain; that, simply as a matter of economy,
it is cheaper to hire labor than to own it; and that, though
he fought to uphold slavery, he is glad that it has been
overthrown.   In this he but says what I have heard from
all Southern men with whom I have conversed.

"And yet this, which you *now* recognize as so great a gain, was the result of war, and, in my judgment, would not have been attained without war. I know how complacently some reason that moral causes would have led to the removal of slavery; but moral causes work very slowly, while the slave population was multiplying fast. I do not believe in the potency of influences which show themselves only in some future generation. On the contrary, many causes combined to strengthen slavery, such as the interest of planters, the habit of mastery, and the pride of a superior over an inferior race. By these influences slavery was becoming more and more imbedded in our national life. The institution, which, at the beginning of this century, was but a sapling, had grown to be a mighty oak, whose roots had struck deep and spread far, and nothing less than the great upheaval of war could wrench it from the American soil.

"The war, then, was inevitable. It had to come; and, since it was a necessity, and since there can not be a war without combatants, without hostile peoples and opposing armies, it may be said in one sense that both wrought to one end. And as the war removed the only cause of difference between the two great sections of our country, it is not too much to say that the blood of the North and the South, shed upon the same battle-fields, has cemented forever an indissoluble Union.

"So much for the great national result. But through what sufferings was this end achieved! Here I would speak with the utmost tenderness. 'Every heart knoweth its own bitterness.' There are wounds which can never be healed, as there are vacant places in our homes which will never be filled. As for the North, God only knows what we suffered. I remember how they used to sing

"'When this cruel war is over,
    The boys will come marching home.'

Alas! many of the boys never came. The mother whose heart was breaking when her son went away, as the months and years rolled by, longed and prayed for his return. In the Summer evening she sat by her window, and asked, 'Why doesn't Charley come?' wondering when she should hear his familiar step and his cheery voice. Alas! she never heard that voice or step again. While she waited and wept and prayed, all that was left of her boy was lying in a nameless grave among the mountains of Virginia.

"Such have been our sorrows, but yours have been even greater, as almost your whole arms-bearing population was in the field; so that sometimes, after a great battle had been fought, it seemed as if the Angel of Death had passed over the land, till, as in the plague of the first-born in Egypt, 'there was not a house in which there was not one dead.' Such sorrows can not be forgotten, they have sunk too deep in the hearts that survive, and can only cease to be felt when those hearts cease to beat. As I look in the faces of Southern women I see no trace of anger, but sometimes an inexpressible sadness, a far-away look, as if their eyes were fixed on some object at a distance, a beloved son or brother, who had gone and would not return. Who of us does not know that look; who has not seen it on the faces of Northern mothers and sisters? Such faces are fewer now than they were soon after the war, for of the greater part death has closed the eyes that were weeping, and the grave has covered the hearts that were broken.

"Of course in those who still live there are memories full of pain, sorrows that should never be touched with an ungentle hand. In Atlanta my friend Mr. Grady invited me to his home, where I saw his mother, a Southern lady of the finest type, who received me with great kindness. 'But,' he said, 'she can not get over the War. *My father was killed at Petersburg!*' Who can say anything to grief such as this? I was silent, but I thought of another who perished there—a brave young captain from my native village, whose name is graven on a humble stone in our cemetery, though his body is not beneath it, for it was buried in the terrible slaughter of ' the crater.' What can we say to these things, but to mourn over the folly and madness which brought such unholy strife, and, in the name of all the beloved dead, endeavor to be more gentle and kind to the living?

" After such bereavements, on one side and on the other, how is it possible for those who have thus suffered to look in the face those whose hands have been lifted against the objects of their dearest affection? I will answer by a single instance, which is a type of thousands. A friend, who long resided in St. Louis, told me recently of a lady of that city who had a son in the Confederate army, that was killed in the war—a sorrow which overshadowed her whole life. So saddened was she by it that she could not visit the North, until at length she was ordered by her physician to a Northern watering-place, where her appearance in deep mourning touched every heart. Especially did it attract a Northern lady, who was unremitting in her attentions to her Southern sister. When the latter was about to leave, she bade her friend good-bye, saying that ' she should never return;' and to the inquiry ' Why?' she answered in a word that told the whole story, ' I lost a son in the war!' Her friend's eyes filled with tears as she replied, ' I too lost a son in the war,' and instantly they threw themselves in each other's arms. At that moment the bitterness of years was blotted out (even though the grief remained) as these two noble women, daughters of the South and the North, were drawn to each other, not only by the ties of womanhood and sisterhood, but by the still stronger tie of a common sorrow.

" If the prize of virtue be given according to the measure of suffering, it must be awarded to the South, which

suffered far more than the North. I know of few things
in history more pathetic than the return of the Southern
soldiers after the war. Those of the North marched back
to their homes in all the pride of victory. When the armies
of Grant and Sherman swept through Pennsylvania avenue
in Washington, under the eye of the President, there was
not a man whose heart did not beat high with the proud
assurance that the cause which he had fought for had been
gained.

"Not so with the veterans of the South. They did not
return as an army, for their military organization was destroyed, but in fragments, worn with the march and the
battle, having fought for years and failed at last. They
came back to the old home perhaps to find it in ashes,
or desolate because of those who had gone out from it
never to return. There was such an exhaustion of the
South that the situation seemed almost hopeless. The
country was ruined. Vast tracts had been ravaged by
hostile armies, and on every hand there had been a degree
of waste and destruction which it seemed as if generations
could not repair. But this very depression only gave fresh
opportunity to show the vitality and energy of the Southern
people. Much as I admire the courage of your soldiers in
the battle-field, I admire still more their spirit when they
confronted this new trial. Facing the desperate situation,
the soldiers of Lee and Stonewall Jackson laid aside their
weapons of war, and put their hardy sinews to the labors
of the field.

"And nobler still, if anything can be nobler, was the
conduct of the matrons and daughters of the South. Even
during the war there was a chivalrous feeling toward them.
We knew how they suffered, and it added to our own
burden of sorrow. Nearly forty years ago I heard Rufus
Choate speak of the attitude of the old Whig party toward
the Mexican War, and I can hear now his rich voice as he

said, ' The wail of the daughters of Mexico and of America
is no music to their ear.' So in the midst of our great
agony, it was only an aggravation to know that all over this
beautiful land of the South there was mourning and lamen-
tation—' Rachel weeping for her children, and that could
not be comforted because they were not.' And when, after
the war, women of gentle birth, who had never known anything but luxury, finding themselves utterly impoverished,
stooped to menial services, such as before had been performed by slaves, the feeling toward them was one of enthusiasm. All honor to these heroic women, who, by their
courage and constancy, showed themselves worthy to be
the mothers of a mighty race!

"And now, thank God! this cruel war is over. Peace
has come, and come to stay. All over this broad land the
sun shines without a cloud. We are one people, having
one country. Underneath all our differences there has
always been a national feeling, which was a constant force,
like gravitation, to bring us together. In that ' funda-
mental law,' not of the Government, but of the great
American heart, we recognize the will of the Almighty that
the North and the South ' should be no more twain but
one flesh,' and ' What God has joined together let not man
put asunder.'

"We do not ask you to forget the past, as we certainly
shall not forget it. Cherish the memory of your heroic
dead, and visit their graves on Decoration-day to cover
them with flowers. Such communion with the dead is instructive to the living. We can not bring them back, but
we can learn the lesson which they teach; and if they
could speak to us, can you doubt that their one request
would be that all bitterness and strife should be buried in
their graves?

"Speaking to soldiers, to Confederate officers, I say to
you what I would say to the distinguished officer of the

United States Army at my left, Follow your leaders!
Could there be a better guide for us all—soldiers and
civilians, North and South—than to follow the counsels of
General Grant and General Lee? We sit here to-night
under the very shadow of a monument" (in the adjoining
square) " lofty as the Column of Trajan at Rome, on which
stands a colossal statue in bronze of your great soldier. As
you pass it day by day, and look up and see that majestic
form outlined against the sky, you remember him as he appeared in the day of battle. Will you not think of him also
when the battle was over? Great as he was in war, he was
greater in peace, when, with his heart full of sorrow, he
retired to his quiet home in Lexington, setting an example
of moderation and self-control truly sublime, and trying to
calm the agitation of his suffering people. To the end of
his days he used all his great influence for peace. ' Do not
train up your children in hostility to the Government of
the United States,' he said to a mother who had been
widowed by the war, and who brought her son to him to be
educated. To these counsels of peace there is a touching
response from the death-chamber of our great soldier,
as he talked with General Buckner most tenderly of
the South, and uttered his dying wish for its full recovery
from all the disasters of the war. Here is a lesson for us.
If we cherish the spirit of General Grant, you can find no
better example than that of General Lee.

"With the Union thus re-established, what a future
opens before our country, growing in population and
wealth as never before! I hear the tread of the millions
that are coming to take possession of this valley. When
this vision is fulfilled; ' when ' (to quote the words of your
own great orator, Sergeant S. Prentiss), ' this Crescent City
shall have filled her golden horns; when in her broad-armed
port shall lie the products of the industry of a hundred
millions of freemen; then may the sons of the Pilgrims,

still wandering from the bleak hills of the North, stand upon the banks of the Great River, and exclaim, Lo! this is our country! When did the world ever witness so rich and magnificent a city; so great and glorious a Republic?' "

As we rose from the table, every Confederate officer present came to me and thanked me for what I had said, and expressed his hearty agreement with it. The response was the same in New Orleans that we had found in Atlanta, in Nashville, and in Montgomery. If the course of remark appear rather grave for the occasion, it was almost unavoidable in the presence of such a company, and the writer, in saying what might draw Northern and Southern hearts together, aimed to act in the true spirit of " a minister of reconciliation."

X.

NEW ORLEANS TO VICKSBURG—SUGAR PLANTATIONS—
BATON ROUGE AND GOV. McENERY—MAJOR BURKE—
VICKSBURG BY MOONLIGHT—MEMORIALS OF THE
SIEGE—THE UNION CEMETERY.

IF anybody has a desire to see Plantation life somewhat
as it used to be in the old days, and as it appeared in
its best estate, he can hardly find it showing to better
advantage anywhere in the South than in the hundred
miles above New Orleans. The Delta of the Mississippi is
like the Delta of the Nile for richness; and even richer,
since it does not depend on the annual overflow of the
Great River to keep up its fertility. Nothing in the Valley
of the Nile can equal these "bottom-lands" of the Mississippi. Here are the great sugar estates, whose owners were
always considered the Southern nabobs. With inexhausti-
ble natural wealth to draw upon, the planters grew rich,
and built the stately mansions which we see, as we look out
of the windows, surrounded with magnolias and orange-
trees, behind which at a distance are the long rows of
white-washed cabins of the negroes. What an Arcadian
picture of peace and plenty, and what a scene for the display of the beauties of the Patriarchial Institution!

In such a country, and with such a climate, slavery
(which is very much a matter of climate) springs up quite
naturally. It is a system which flourishes most in hot
climates, where the very temperature disposes the superior
race to take life easily, and to impose the burden of labor
upon others. In Africa itself slavery seems to be a product of the burning heat as much as the palms on the

desert. And so here it seemed to agree well with this half-
African climate and this half-tropical vegetation. The
superficial traveller is very apt to take such a view of the
fitness of things, and, as he rides over a country "where it
is always afternoon," and feels its soft languor creeping
over him, he almost regrets the absence of an institution
which made life so easy that it moved on without friction
or worry of any kind; in which the planter (who is of
course supposed to have been always generous and indulgent) was truly the patriarch of his large family, the protector as well as proprietor of his people, under whose
gentle rule they lived and died with the minimum of labor
and without a particle of care!

But with all the poetry and the sunshine that can be put
into slavery, there were connected with it some possibilities
which one can not contemplate with a tranquil mind.
"Papa," said a little fellow who was born since the war,
"Did you ever *own* my old Mammy?" "Yes, my son;
but why do you ask?" "Do you mean that you owned
her *just as you own 'Daisy'*?"—a favorite horse. The
father could not deny it. "And that you could sell her
just as you could sell 'Daisy'?" "Yes." The child
made no reply, but went away dazed by a thought which
put his manly little heart in fierce rebellion. And it set
his father (who was a very kind-hearted man) thinking
too! As he afterward confessed to a friend, "He had
never thought of slavery exactly in that light." The pos-
sibility of selling the old nurse of his child—one who had
loved that boy as his own mother—struck him as never before, and he inwardly gave thanks that such horrors could
no more be enacted in the sight of heaven.

Those who predicted ruin to this beautiful country if slavery were abolished will be disappointed (I hope not pained)
to find that the country "still lives," and is apparently as
flourishing as ever. If here and there an old planter, dis-

gusted at the emancipation of his slaves, has forsaken the
place of his birth, he did not carry it away with him: " he
left the land behind," and the strong hands to till it, so
that his deserted people might " cheer up " by singing
Whittier's " Song of the Negro Boatmen ":

> " Ole massa on his trabbels gone;
>   He leab de land behind;
> De Lord's breff blow him furder on,
>   Like corn-shuck in de wind!
> De yam will grow, de cotton blow;
>   We'll hab de rice and corn;
> Oh nebber you fear if nebber you hear
>   De driver blow his horn!"

But many of the old planters did not desert " the old
home," but stood by it, and now they or their children
reap the reward. To be sure, slavery is gone; the land is
no more owned by masters and tilled by slaves; but the
same population is here, though the two classes into which
it is divided stand in different relations to each other. If
you say simply planter instead of master, and laborer instead of bondman, you have the same men still standing in
the relation of employer and employed. The same work
goes on, and the earth yields her increase as before; and
wherever the present owners have the tact to use free labor
wisely, they find it quite as profitable as slave labor, and
by it they have restored much of their old-time prosperity,
and retained in their families the proud inheritance of the
old " manors " on which their fathers lived and died.

After running North some hundred and thirty miles we
came to the foot of a bluff overlooking the river, which was
conspicuous at a distance, the more so because crowned
with a marble structure, which looked like what it is—a
State House. We were at Baton Rouge, the capital of
Louisiana. Here we halted to pay our respects to another
Governor. We were marched up the hill, and ushered into

the Capitol, where a gentleman of rather slight figure, perhaps sixty years of age, was standing to receive us. While we were being presented in due form, a number of persons, officials of the State House and others, had crowded into the room; and before we could retire, a voice with which I had become familiar suggested that "Dr. Field would make a few remarks!" Though taken by surprise, I said what I could on the spur of the moment, not hesitating to speak frankly about the war and "our common country," to which the Governor (who, I take for granted, was an old soldier, since nobody else has a chance of being elected to any office in the South) responded in as loyal a tone as one could wish to hear. And when we turned to leave a dozen hands were stretched out with a hearty grip, which said more plainly than words that they too agreed with me. The Governor then took my arm and accompanied us down to our car. So far as one could judge from this *long* acquaintance of a few minutes, he seemed a very quiet, pleasant-spoken gentleman, which surprised me a little, as I had somehow got the idea that he was a terrible "fire-eater!" Governor McEnery had been very much criticised in New Orleans because of a supposed wish to spare a couple of men who had shot another in cold blood, and had been tried and condemned to death. As the quarrel grew out of some political feud, party feeling was enlisted, and there was a strong effort to have their sentence commuted; and it was said that the Governor had favored the movement by reprieving the men, and thus delaying the execution. But, as since we left he has issued his death-warrant, and *they have been hung*, there is nothing more to be said on the subject.

When we received the Governor on our special train, I hope he was duly impressed with awe, as we were when ushered into his august presence in the State House; for we were travelling to-day with a little more state than usual.

A new road had recently been opened, parallel to the Mississippi, from New Orleans to Memphis—a road built by New York capitalists, one of whom was in our party, and we were making a sort of trial-trip over it. The Vice-President had come down from Memphis to see to our comfort, and attached *his* President's car to *our* President's car, which gave increased magnificence to the turn-out with which we were making our royal progress through the country. If it is a distinction for a traveller to have one car to himself, it is double glory to have *two*. With this new arrangement, our own car was made to serve merely as a dining-room, while in the other we "spread ourselves" over the luxurious sofas, and had the double pleasure of the outlook and the conversation as we rushed through cane-brake and forest, with glimpses of the river on one side, and of rich plantations on the other.

The enjoyment of the day was much increased by the addition to our party of Major Burke, to whom I have referred once or twice. He came into the St. Charles at New Orleans just as we were leaving, and we captured him on the spot, and carried him off "a prisoner," and took him as far as Vicksburg, from which he could return in the night train, so as to be at his desk early the next morning. He has had a remarkable life. During the war he was a Confederate officer. Since then he has fought two or three duels, just to keep his hand in; but I am glad to say, in neither did he kill his antagonist, and of course he would not be killed himself, for he has as many lives as a cat. A dashing soldier, he is at the same time a most agreeable talker. Where he is, conversation can never be dull. He can tell stories not only of the war, but of the times after the war, when Louisiana was under the rule of the carpet-baggers: and gave us an inside view of the politics of the State. He is a warm personal friend of Governor McEnery, whose delay in ordering the execution of

the men in New Orleans he explained as but a proper deference to public opinion.

But nothing interested me so much as his experiment of
skilled negro labor, which grew out of the necessities of
war. Being attached to that portion of the Confederate
army which was beyond the Mississippi, he found it suffering greatly from want of transportation—of horses, of sad-
dles and bridles, and harnesses and baggage-wagons. If
horses were injured on the march there was nothing to do
but to shoot them, as there was no place of cure to which
they could be sent and cared for till they were fit to take
their places in the field again. The difficulty in procuring
proper equipments was still greater. There was a want of
skilled labor for all this kind of handicraft. The white
carpenters, and wagon-makers, and blacksmiths, and sad-
dle- and harness-makers, were already drafted for the army.
In this extremity, he conceived the idea of taking the
negroes, and converting them into skilled workmen. It
did not seem a very promising experiment, but he undertook it. Of course he did not take the common run of
field hands, but picked out those who were most intelligent
and capable, strong of limb and quick of wit; and with
such materials he made excellent workmen, and established
a large manufactory of war material in the interior of
Texas, where it would not be likely to be interrupted by an
attack from the Northern army; while the old war-horses,
instead of being shot, were led off into pastures, where they
could slowly recover strength, so that their necks should be
" clothed with thunder " when the sound of the trumpet
called them to battle again. It was certainly a notable experiment, which showed at once the capacity of the negro,
and the wonderful skill and energy of the man who conceived this bold scheme, and carried it out so successfully—
a power of organization which he showed a few years later
in organizing the Great Exposition at New Orleans.

While listening to these reminiscences of the past, which may help to solve a problem of the future in regard to the fitness of the negro for a higher occupation than that of digging the soil, we caught the name of a place which had an historic interest. It was Port Gibson, near which is the landing of Grand Gulf, at which General Grant (after his boats had run the gauntlet of the batteries at Vicksburg) crossed the Mississippi with his army. A few minutes later we gathered on the platform to look up and down the Big Black from the height of the long bridge which spans it—a river which appears constantly in the military reports of the day. The story was all in mind as it is told by the great soldier himself in "The Century Magazine" with the utmost clearness, while at the same time with the utmost simplicity and modesty. As the eye ranged over the country which was the scene of that immortal campaign, we could imagine the imperturbable chief pushing inland, and, as it were, burning his ships behind him, to cast the fate of his army on the fate of a battle; fighting from day to day, now at Champion Hills, and now on other bloody fields, till he had forced Pemberton back into his intrench-ments, and the great siege was begun.

It was dark when we entered Vicksburg. As we were to spend the night in our cars, we had not prepared to disem-bark. But hardly had we come to a stand-still when we were suddenly "invaded" with hospitable intent. The Confederates were upon us, and there was nothing to do for it but to surrender gracefully, at least so far as to en-gage to spend an hour at the house of a well-known gentle-man, to exchange kindly greetings with our new friends. But I was so eager to see the place that I could not come under any man's roof until I had first taken a general sur-vey of the town. So muffling up in a thick overcoat, for the evening air was chill, I attached myself to an old resi-dent who had been here during the siege, and begged him to lead the way. It was a beautiful night. The full moon shone down on city and river. He took me first to the levee which slopes down to the landing, while behind us rose a long line of hills. As we looked out upon the broad surface of the mighty stream, gliding softly and peacefully in the moonlight, I could not but contrast the scene with that of the night when our fleet ran through a mile of the batteries planted alike at the water's edge and along the crest of the hills. Of course the commander did not choose such a night as this, when all his movements would be exposed as in the light of day. Naturally he would wish to take a night that was pitch-dark, that his movement might be concealed; and I had pictured him in my fancy as dropping down the river silently, as with muffled oar. But I soon saw that this was impossible. A Mississippi steamboat is not easily muffled; it has a snort like a war-horse that smells the battle from afar, and the revolution of its wheels may be heard at a great distance. Besides, the movement had been anticipated, and watch had been kept by night as well as by day; and no sooner was the fleet in motion than an old house on the opposite bank was set on fire, so that the river was suddenly lighted with a glare that revealed every object for miles, and thus every boat was a mark as soon as she came within range. On a high point of the bluff at the upper end of the city, the Confederates had planted a huge gun, which from its screeching sound had been christened "Whistling Dick," and there they kept watch for the steamers, which had to round a point of land right opposite, by which their broadsides were exposed to its fire. As the "Cincinnati" was turning the corner a shot plunged into her, and she sunk instantly. But her fate did not deter her consorts, which kept steadily onward. As the whole fleet came into line in the channel of the river they were exposed to a terrific fire, as all the batteries on the hills belched forth shot and flame. That they were not annihilated seems a miracle. But they put on full steam, and in a short time had passed the point of danger. The means of transportation were secured, so that when General Grant marched his army by land down the west bank of the river to a point far below Vicksburg, he had the means of crossing to where the great business of war was to begin.

"It must have been rather a hot time you had during the siege," I said to my companion.

"Wall, it *was* rather a wakeful time: we didn't get much sleep them days, nor nights either, but after a while we got kinder used to it, and would go down into the cellars, or crawl into the holes in the sides of the bluff, and sleep there."

"Are those holes still remaining? I should like to see them."

"They have mostly caved in, or been filled up; but you can see some of 'em."

With that we climbed the hill, and near the top my guide pointed out a number of pits in which the people had taken refuge. Those into which I crept were mere swallow-holes in a sand-bank, enlarged to the size of a man, though I should think it must have been pretty hard for a six-footer to stretch himself in one of them. At the time of the siege some of these "dug-outs" were quite large. The hill-side, being of soft earth, was easily excavated, and by dig-ging away for a day or two, one might get to himself a subterranean chamber, where the earth above him formed a cushion for any stray shells that might descend upon it. At best they must have been stifling places in those hot Summer days (Vicksburg surrendered on the Fourth of July); but at night they were cooler, and one who crawled in here, and literally

"Laid his head upon a lap of earth,"

might rest in quietness for a few hours, without the fear of being blown into eternity.

On the top of the hill stood the Court House like a high tower, and being the most conspicuous object in the town, was a mark for the enemy's guns. On the other side of the river, one of our gunners, who had a " Parrott " of which he was as proud as a hunter of his favorite rifle, thought he would try his hand on the cupola, and " drew a bead " on it, determined to ring the bell! But though he fired perhaps hundreds of times, his shots went over or sidewise, and whatever execution they may have done elsewhere, they did not hit the mark. Once indeed he carried away a pillar of the cupola, but did not make the bell ring! It was not to be rung by cannon-balls, but by human hands in the happy days of peace that were to come.

" But look here!" said my guide as we passed a Methodist church, pointing to the rear wall, in which a piece of shell was lodged during the siege, perhaps to remain as long as the ball fired from the British fleet remained in the belfry of the Old South Church in Boston. I knew that my Methodist brethren were given to sensations, and liked to be " roused up," but I doubted whether any preacher had produced by his eloquence such an awakening as did the crashing of that shell into the side of their house of worship.

It appears strange that people could go to church at all at such a time. We can not understand how life should go on as before, for it seems as if all ordinary duties and occupations would be paralyzed by the universal terror. But such is the power of repetition to dull the senses that after a while men get deadened to pain and to fear, so that they take up again almost mechanically the common round of life. They become so used to danger that they can to some extent go about their affairs as if it did not exist. And so it was that churches were opened and sermons preached during that time of horror.

A gentleman who rode about with us the next day, told me that his wife was on her way to the Catholic church one Sunday morning, when she stopped at the door to speak to an old gentleman, and while they spoke a cannon-ball fell between them, and carried off his hand! She immediately bound up the arm with the help of her brother, and he was taken home, while she entered the church to perform her devotions. In the midst of the service a ball crashed through the ceiling over her head, whereupon the priest, who was performing the mass, concluded abruptly and dismissed the congregation, who did not stand upon the order of their going, but retreated to their caves in the sides of the hills.

From these memories of war it was pleasant to turn to the smiling face of peace, that greeted us as we came to a large mansion gayly lighted up, which we entered to receive the warmest welcome. After an hour spent with those who treated us, not as new acquaintances but as old friends, we strode down the hill in the moonlight, to the spacious car which served us as a floating hotel.

But morning had hardly gleamed on the river when I was out on the bluff to take in the whole scene by daylight. There it lay below us, with every feature outlined as distinctly as on a map—the river making a great bend upward to Vicksburg, and inclosing a narrow peninsula, across the neck of which Grant tried to dig a canal for his boats without success. But what man could not do the river itself has done, bursting a passage through by the force of its mighty current, and wearing a channel broad and deep; while it has retired from Vicksburg to such extent that she lies now almost stranded, like an old hulk on a sandbank, and willows are growing in the midst of the old channel!

As soon as we could despatch breakfast, carriages were waiting to give us a drive. Turning southward, we rode

along the bluff for a mile or two to take in the position of
the city as related to the river and the surrounding country.   After scanning with eager eyes every point on both
sides of the river, we faced about and took in the circuit of
the hills.   The country behind Vicksburg is broken, ridges
alternating with deep gullies—a country which is at once
difficult of approach and easy of defence.   One glance
showed us how small and petty had been our idea of the
siege, as if it were confined within the space of a square
mile, whereas the Confederate batteries were mounted on
yonder hills more than a mile away, while Grant's army,
making a still larger circuit to inclose the former, must
have stretched from the point where it touched the river on
the south to where it touched it on the north, over a distance of ten or twelve miles, thus coiling round and round
like a mighty serpent, winding itself closer and closer, till
the beleaguered city was literally strangled in its tremendous folds.

Then riding slowly backward through the city, which has
such a historic name, we came out at the northern end,
where, on a hill-side, gleam the white stones of the Union
Cemetery.   Our train had followed us, and waited for us
on the track below, while we climbed the hill to pay our
homage to the heroic dead.   As the Siege of Vicksburg
lasted for two months, and was preceded by a series of battles, there was literally an army of the dead, whose remains
were afterward gathered reverently and tenderly from the
fields where they fell, and placed in their last resting-place.
The Cemetery is laid out with much taste, and kept as carefully as Greenwood, though it has no such splendid monu-
ments, nor such variety of architectural ornament: for of the
sixteen thousand whose bones are gathered here, less than
four thousand names are known!   Hence they could only
be laid side by side with their companions-in-arms; and so
they lie in successive rows and squares, ranks on ranks, a

low head-stone at each grave the only mark of " a soldier's sepulchre." These are the unknown dead! But though their names be not preserved by history, their deeds will be held in everlasting remembrance. They did not die in vain: for by their blood they preserved to us the priceless blessing of Union and Liberty. And long as yonder river rolls its majestic flood to the sea, will a grateful country remember those who died that she might live!

XI.

VICKSBURG is a hard place to get out of one's mind: it has too many warlike memories. That cemetery on the hill-side I shall never forget, though we saw it only in the broad daylight, which is not the time when we feel most the power of the associations of such a spot. What must it be at night, when the wind stirs gently in the pines that murmur their soft requiem for the dead, and the full moon, sinking in the west, silvers the broad expanse of the Mississippi, and striking across it, touches with a pale and tender light the low head-stones that mark sixteen thousand graves! Peace to the " unreturning brave!"

But a few minutes after we had left this place of sacred memories, we were standing on the platform, to catch a glimpse, as we passed, of a large house on the bluff above us, which was General Grant's head-quarters during the siege. It must have been nearly at the northern extremity of the long semicircle which he drew around the doomed city. Three or four miles further—ten miles above Vicksburg—we crossed the Yazoo, which is a large river, navigable by steamboats. It was by the ascent of this river that the great soldier made his first attempt to get in the rear of Vicksburg, and only when defeated in this, that he tried to cut a canal across the peninsula in front of the city; and failing in that also, that he formed the daring resolution to run the gauntlet of the Confederate batteries, and finally succeeded in getting the transports for his army at the point where he wished them, a long distance below the city.

The bridge which now spans the Yazoo is one of the finest in all the South: over nine hundred feet long, built of iron, resting on stone piers, and corresponds in its massive solidity to the magnificent railroad of which it is a part (that from New Orleans to Memphis, a distance of 455 miles)—an iron track which has been but recently completed, but which is as solid in its road-bed, and over which the wheels run as smoothly, as over many of the oldest roads of the North.

Though we see no trace of the great events of which this country was the theatre, and not the faintest vestige of military occupation, we are glad to find here and there a Northern officer, who since the war has made his home in the South.   One of General Thomas's most trusted commanders has fixed his residence at Chattanooga, and I am told is enthusiastic in his praise of that picturesque region. And here, fifty-three miles above Vicksburg, we passed a large plantation, owned and cultivated by Dr. Phelps, the Surgeon-General of Grant's army, who finds himself quite at home in the South, and as happy in growing cotton in Mississippi as he would be in growing wheat in Illinois or Ohio.

We are now in the Delta between the Yazoo and the Mississippi—one of the richest cotton regions in the world. The land is especially adapted to produce cotton, yielding in some cases a bale to the acre, which is considered a very large product.   The quality too is of such a grade that it brings from an eighth to a quarter of a cent a pound more in the market at Liverpool than most of the cottons of the South, and indeed excels them all with the single exception of the sea-island cotton, grown off the coast of the Carolinas.

At Leland, eighty miles north of Vicksburg, a branch road diverges to the Lake Washington Country, and another to Huntington on the Mississippi, where it connects with a road on the other side of the river in Arkansas, leading to Little Rock and Fort Smith. These branches are feeders to the trunk line. At the point of junction a large station is placed conveniently in the angle of the roads, at which travellers from different directions meet and dine together, bow across the table, and depart.

The "crack" plantation of all this country is that to which its owner, Mr. Forgason, has given the pretty name of "Clover Hill," though it shows more cotton than clover. It is seventy miles below Memphis, and about fifteen miles back from the river. As our train swept through it, we saw the manager riding about on horseback to look after the extensive estate under his care. What especially attracted our attention was the ample quarters provided for the negro laborers, which showed a proper consideration for their comfort. We were sorry not to be able to stop and pay a visit to this model plantation. The owner, who lives in Memphis, came to call on our party, and it was a pleasure to take by the hand one who is a representative of that new race of planters which is to make the New South richer and happier than the Old.

But it must not be supposed that this cotton region is a monotonous plain, like some of our Northern prairies, unbroken by forest or stream. On the contrary, it is well watered by "creeks" and dotted with lakes; and not unfrequently we pass from the broad sunshine of a plantation, where the men at the plough

> " Jocund drive the team a-field,"

into the deep shadows of the woods, or into a tract grown up with the wild cane, whose long and graceful stems reminded me of the bamboos of India. Once we stopped in the midst of a cane-brake, that our party might supply themselves with fishing-rods cut by their own hands. Had there been time for such diversions, they might have had abundance of sport in this very region. Deer are found in the woods, and it is said that a hunter who plunges into the dense thicket of the cane may sometimes stir up a bear who makes a haunt of the reeds and rushes. Forty-five miles south of Memphis is Beaver Dam Lake—a beautiful sheet of water, on the shore of which has been built a Club House for sportsmen, that is a favorite resort of those who are fond of fishing or hunting. Nearer to the city is Lake View, which is to Memphis what Coney Island is to New York—a cool retreat in the heat of Summer.

It was four o'clock when we drew up in front of Memphis. We found it, like Vicksburg, on the bank of the Great River, though not perched on a hill-side, but spreading out over a more level surface and to much greater extent. I could only wish that those who settled the place, when they christened it, had had the good sense to give it one of the musical Indian names which we found scattered along our route; or one which might have some local significance, if it were only to preserve the name of the first white inhabitant, as Vicksburg was named from the family of Vick (whose descendants still live in the old house, that was pointed out to us), instead of going to Egypt, and taking the name of the capital of the Pharaohs for a town on the Mississippi! But "what's in a name?" There is much in a name, and it ought always to have some degree of appropriateness; but Memphis might as well have been baptized by the name of Belshazzar or Nebuchadnezzar as by that of the ancient city on the Nile. We were much better pleased with the name of our Hotel, the "Gayoso House:" for "Gayoso" is Indian, and so is native American, instead of being Egyptian, which is African. But while the name is Indian, there is nothing of the wigwam in the Hotel, which is one of the very best that we have found in all the South; and the town itself, though Egyp-

tian in name, is pure American in character, and an excellent specimen of an American city.

It was a pleasant change from the regulation dinner, with
speeches, which had been the usual ending of each day, that
this evening we were all invited to a wedding-party, not to
witness a marriage ceremony, which might have been in a
church, but to a reception given in honor of *three* married
couples at the house of Colonel Montgomery, the father of
one of the brides. It was a mile or two back from the
river, yet the city is built up the whole distance. Where
the business portion ends, the residences begin, and very
beautiful they are, as they are generally set back from the
street, and stand in the midst of lawns and gardens, with
every indication of the wealth and taste of their occupants.

The occasion was peculiar in being given for three brides,
who had been married at about the same time—it may
have been on the same day—and who therefore united in
this joint reception to their common friends. One of these
was a granddaughter of President Andrew Johnson. All
stood together under a bower of roses, beaming with happiness, and received the congratulations of the guests. The
occasion brought together a large and distinguished company. At one moment we were introduced to a learned
judge; the next to a lawyer, whose reputation is not confined to his own city or State; now to a Member of Congress,
familiar with the society of Washington; and now to the editor of " The Memphis Appeal," or " Avalanche "—papers
which are known throughout the country. The ladies were
all brightness and gayety. Among them was a daughter of
the famous Admiral Semmes of the " Alabama," in whom,
as in others present, there was a cordiality of manner
peculiar to the South, and which gives a great charm to
the best Southern society. I am not in the habit of comparing society in one place with that in another; but I could
not perceive much difference between this reception and a

similar one in New York. Wherever in the world you
bring together "fair women and brave men," there is
society. I was reminded of a remark which Mrs. Harriet
Beecher Stowe made to me after her return from England,
where she had seen much of high life, and been fêted by
lords and ladies, whom many suppose to be very assuming
and pretentious because of their rank, but of whom she
said that she found them "just like the nicest people in
our own country;" that from the very fact that they had
an assured position, they had the most unassuming manners. Such men and women do not belong exclusively to
any class or country: they are the rich inheritance of all
highly civilized nations. In our own country, they may be
found alike in the North and the South. If this evening's
gathering were a fair representation of the society of Memphis, it must be a very agreeable city to live in.

The next morning we were driven round the town by the
Mayor and a delegation of citizens, among whom was Mr.
Thomas H. Allen, who has been a successful merchant here
for the past fifty years. We were surprised at the extent
of the city and its business activity. Memphis is one of the
greatest cotton marts in the South. It is in the line of the
Cotton Belt, which stretches from east to west, and on both
sides of the Mississippi, cotton being brought in large quantities from Arkansas to Memphis as the most convenient
point for shipment. To prepare it for this, we found here as
at Atlanta, that the first necessity was that it be " com-
pressed " to reduce its bulk, and this in itself is a large and
profitable industry. Col. Montgomery, our host of the last
evening, is at the head of the most extensive compressing es-
tablishment; and here again we watched the operation of the
iron monster, which takes up the big, bulging, bloated bales,
and squeezes them till all their " starch " is taken out of
them, and they lie as flat as so many pancakes. Next we
entered a factory for expressing the oil from cotton-seed,

and by the way it kept oozing out, and falling drip, drip, into the pans below, we judged that the yield was sufficient, not only to grease innumerable wheels, and make all kinds of machinery run smoothly, but to supply "oleomargarine" for the whole Southern country.

But Memphis was first laid out, not so much for a manufacturing as a commercial city, its position on the Mississippi giving it facilities for trade up and down through twenty degrees of latitude. It is still a port of entry, as one may see by the Custom House, built of stone, which stands high up on the bluff, overlooking both town and river; and by the stately steamers which are floating up and down. But a portion of the traffic is being diverted to the railroads. It seemed a bold movement on the part of the newly constructed line from Memphis to New Orleans to "run opposition to the Mississippi river;" but the issue has justified it, as it transported the very first year several hundred thousand bales of cotton, and the amount must increase from year to year. Of course transportation by water is cheaper than by land, but it is subject to many contingencies. The Mississippi is an unruly monster: it is like a wild horse, which, when he "takes the bit in his teeth," is hard to check or to guide. As the factories which we have just been visiting stand on the bank, supported partly by piles, we went to the rear to look out upon the river, and found it coming frightfully near. Although the Spring flood had but just begun, the current was sweeping against the bank with great violence, here and there washing it away, so that it must soon be a question whether the factories shall not be removed to higher ground, or piles be driven thicker and deeper, and filled in with blocks of granite, to secure a permanent foundation. In looking at the map, I have often been puzzled by the windings of the Great River, which are like the contortions of a serpent in pain, writhing and twisting in its agony, and tried to discover the final cause of this—how it was done and *what it was for*. Now, as I watch it and see its destructive power, I can not but look upon it as a provision of Nature or of Providence (call it which you please) to preserve the country from destruction: for if the Mississippi were to flow in a straight line from its head-waters to the Gulf, it would acquire such velocity and momentum, that it would sweep away the country on its banks, and carry millions of acres of the richest land in the world into the sea.

After we had thus taken a general survey of the city and its surroundings, we returned to our car to take our departure. Our friends were with us to bid us farewell, and Mayor Hadden " improved the occasion " to offer a few remarks. In these he enlarged on the growth of Memphis in the last few years, and the great future to which it was destined. He welcomed the opening of each new railroad which made this city its terminus, as it brought more business and more wealth. Across the Mississippi were other railroads traversing another State, and reaching out their long arms into other regions of equal fertility. Why should these two divisions of the Great Valley be separated? At St. Louis a bridge had been built, so that trains from the East and the West rolled across without unloading a single car. Why should not Memphis have the same addition to its present facilities? That was the one thing needed, and it was sure to come. " The next time you visit our city," said the Mayor, raising himself to his full height (and he is a tall man), " you will see a magnificent bridge spanning yonder river. And—and—Gentlemen " [here he paused to make his words emphatic] " WE EXPECT YOU TO PAY FOR IT!" This was received with a shout of applause, and from the remarks I heard afterward I do not think it would be difficult to raise, even among the members of our own party, the necessary sum (only a trifle of two or three

5

millions) to build it. Welcome the day! And may we all be there to ride over it!

But just now we are to ride in another direction. Our iron horse has been standing on the track for several hours, "champing at the bit," and as we let him go, his head is turned to the north-east, making straight for Louisville on the Ohio. But it is a long ride, and (as Memphis is in the extreme south-west corner of Tennessee, not far from the Mississippi line) the distance that we shall make by daylight will be within the State of Tennessee, of which I have a few parting words to say before we cross the border into Kentucky. It is with States as with men: some are overrated, and some are underrated; some pass for less than they are worth, and some for a great deal more. Judging States by a fair test, it seems to me that Tennessee has not had justice done to her, either in history or in public opinion. We hear a great deal about Virginia, though less now than a generation ago, when she was the Old Dominion, the Mother of Presidents. Then South Carolina, in the days of Calhoun, stepped to the front as the defender of Southern institutions, the leader in a war which was to grind her to the dust; and behind her stood Georgia, the "Empire State of the South;" and Louisiana; and Texas, which is truly an empire in itself; while further North, Kentucky, the home of Henry Clay, was regarded as possessing the flower of Southern chivalry. But Tennessee, sandwiched between Kentucky and Georgia and Alabama, was somewhat overlooked. And yet Tennessee has given three Presidents to the Union, while from all the rest of the South appears only one other name for more than sixty years—that of Gen. Zachary Taylor. Wherefore she need not be at all abashed in the presence of her ambitious neighbors. Indeed it appears to me that, in the whole sisterhood of Southern States, there is not one more worthy to lift up her head than good old Tennessee.

Certainly not one has a more central or commanding
position. Tennessee is, geographically, a part of the Great
Valley. Not only is her western border formed by the
Mississippi, but her great rivers, the Tennessee and the
Cumberland, which flow northward, empty into the Ohio,
and thus find their way back into the "Amazon of North
America" that drains all tributaries from the Alleghanies
to the Rocky Mountains. But for all this, Tennessee is not
so exclusively a River State as some others—Mississippi, for
instance, or Arkansas, or Louisiana—for her territory
reaches half way to the Atlantic, and she lies stretched out
on the face of the country, like a sleeping giant, with her
feet dipped in the waters of the Great River, while her head
rests majestically in the lap of the Eastern mountains.

Thus she has every variety of surface and scenery. Eastern Tennessee is one of the most picturesque portions of
our whole country. As the mountains of Virginia are continued south-westward along the line that separates Tennessee from the Carolinas, and reach out far on either side,
those who are familiar with the beauties of the Blue Ridge
and the Shenandoah Valley, will find these repeated in
Eastern Tennessee. And yet this region is little known to
Northern excursionists, who make their annual visits to the
White Hills of New Hampshire, and seem not to know anything of a region of equal attraction, which is hardly
twenty-four hours from New York. Now that a novelist
has appeared in the person of a Southern lady, who has laid
the scene of her stories in the Great Smoky Mountains of
Tennessee, which she describes with the touch of a landscape painter, it is to be hoped that the lovers of the picturesque will turn their steps in that direction. If we had a
friend who was fond of riding on horseback, and looking
about for some untravelled region in which to take his
Summer excursion, we should advise him to take his way
to Eastern Tennessee, where he might pass a few weeks de-

lightfully, riding over the ridges, and coming down into the valleys which lie between—a constant succession of mountain and valley, which will remind him of many beautiful pictures in the Tyrol.

Possessed of such a territory, the population of Tennessee has proved itself worthy of its splendid domain. At the time of the Revolutionary War, Tennessee was a part of North Carolina, and was largely settled from that State. Before the sons of New England pushed through the forest to the Lakes, the backwoodsmen of the Carolinas, clad in buckskin, with axe and gun, were slowly making their way over the mountains. These pioneers were hardy and brave, facing the dangers of wild beasts and more savage men. Wherever the woodman came, he cut away with his axe a little clearing in the forest to let in the sunlight, and with the trees that he felled he built a log cabin—his first home in the wilderness.

Among the early settlers of the Carolinas, there was a strong Scotch-Irish element, like that which peopled Western Pennsylvania. These men were not outcasts from the Old Country: they left it because it was not worthy to retain them. Some of them had fought at the siege of Londonderry, and all were imbued with the ardor of religious liberty, and, like the Pilgrim Fathers, sought a New World that they might have freedom to worship God. The sons of these men who emigrated to Tennessee were not renegades from society—adventurers seeking to escape from the restraints of civilization. Wherever they came they carried the Ark of God with them. The smoke which might have been seen in those days far off on a mountain side, curling upward in the morning air, was but an emblem of the incense of prayer which went up from the dwellers beneath. A God-fearing family in the wilderness was the seed-corn of civilization: for where the log cabin had been built, and a few settlers gathered round, the log school-house followed, and soon the log meeting-house nestled at their side, and these were the elements of a Christian community. Such men were worthy to be the founders of a State—of a great, free, Christian Commonwealth.

The impress of those noble fathers is still seen in their children to the third and fourth generation. The little settlement in the woods has grown into a village, and the village perhaps into a city; and with the increase of population and material wealth, there has been a corresponding growth of institutions of education and religion. The log school-house has been the germ of the Common-School system—which extends its blessing, not only to every large town, but to every village and hamlet—as well as of the splendid institutions which crown the hill-tops round the city of Nashville; while the log meeting-house has been the germ of hundreds of churches, whose spires pointing to heaven show the religious character of the people.

But my pen is running away with me, and I must stop. While I have been "a-thinking" after this sort, our train has been running swiftly to the North, and as we come to the border of Kentucky, I turn to the State we leave behind, and, applying to her the words with which the Governor of Massachusetts always ended his Thanksgiving Proclamation, I say, "God bless the Commonwealth of Tennessee!"

XII.

A VISIT to the South ends when the traveller, on his
return, reaches the banks of the Ohio—the old border-line
between the Free and the Slave States. Here then we have
come to the winding up of our story, in which we shall
pay our respects to Kentucky, as we have paid them to
Tennessee.

When we walked up the steps and into the broad hall of
the Galt House in Louisville, we found ourselves in as comfortable a Hotel as one needs to find in any city of the land,
North or South. Here, as everywhere that we had been,
we had a fresh taste of Southern hospitality. As usual, it
was all Mr. Inman's doing. Nobody knew us, but many
knew him, and for his sake we were treated as "of the
family." He is connected with Louisville in a business
way. This city is the head-quarters of one of the great railway systems of the United States, which takes its name
from the two cities of Louisville and Nashville, which it
was first formed to connect, but which is no longer limited
to the distance between them, but reaches out a hand to its
sister city on the Ohio, Cincinnati: and another to St.
Louis, on the Mississippi; and through these points (together with its own center, Louisville) connects with
twenty-two trunk lines to the East; while beyond St. Louis,

it reaches away to Kansas City on the extreme border of Missouri. But its chief development has been in the Southwest, in which direction it extends to New Orleans, and has leased other roads which it did not own, that it might bring them all under one control, until, in the flowery language of a Southern eulogist, " it stretches its Briarean arms over thirteen States, and joins with bands of steel the waters of the Lakes to the orange groves of the Gulf." Of this company, Mr. Inman and Mr. Rutter are Directors; and hence the President and those of the Directors who live in Louisville, were early on hand to show us attentions, which included a luncheon at the Pendennis Club. As this was a company of business men, it was hardly to be expected that there would be any other talking than in the way of conversation, and I thought I should escape this time; but as we were about to rise from the table, there came round a note written in " that fine Roman hand " with which I had become so familiar, saying that " a few remarks would be in order," and that I must remember that this was a gathering of railroad men, and whatever was said should be in view of that fact. This was not only setting me going again, but switching me off on a new track.

Having a subject thus given me, I made such response as I could, saying (what was not mere compliment, but sincere conviction) that railroads are the pioneers of civilization; that they do more for the development of a country than almost any other single agency. The growth of our country, great as it might still have been from other causes, had been immensely accelerated by the stimulus of these national roads, which plowed up the prairies, and cut their way through the forest, penetrating the wilderness, " where no man was," and there opened new regions for the habitations of men.

This good effect of railroads was entirely independent of

the motives of the builders. Such enterprises were not set
on foot as a work of benevolence, but as a matter of
business, as men engage in any other lawful occupation.
But no matter for that. Even though their projectors
might have been animated only by sordid and selfish
motives, they "builded better than they knew," and in
the end the country at large reaped the benefit of the
great works which they completed. The men passed
away, but the works remained to be the inheritance of
after generations.

In our country railroads had a political as well as commercial value. They, and they only, could prevent our
Union of States from becoming unwieldy the larger it grew,
and dropping apart by the fact of its enormous extension.
That would have been our greatest danger, had not these
roads, keeping pace with the increase of population, or a
little in advance of it, reached out to each new State and
Territory, connecting it at once with the seat of government, and with the long-settled and populous States, and
so bound all parts of the country together. Thus the
Union had grown, not from without, but from within; not
suddenly and violently by acquisitions of new territory, but
by the safe process of gradual increase, till it had crossed
the continent, stretching its mighty expanse from the broad
Atlantic to the broader Pacific.

Nor was this all that was to be said for railroads and
their builders. What they had done for our country, they
would do for other countries. I had seen what English
railroads had done in India: Russian railroads were now
penetrating Central Asia: and wherever they came, they
would prove agencies of civilization. The great men of
modern times were not soldiers, but engineers; not the
captains of armies, but the captains of industry; who were
reconstructing the face of the earth; by whose gigantic
labors " the valleys were exalted and the hills were made

low," to the end, as I fully believed, of "casting up a high-way for the coming of the Lord."

Having run into this moral strain, I could not but say one word (as it was the last I could say in the South) of the Country that was so dear to us all—dearer than ever by the sufferings through which she had passed; lately torn asunder by civil war, but now at last happily reunited, and bound together, not only with bands of iron, but by millions of loyal and loving hearts; and which we devoutly prayed might remain forever "one and inseparable."

This I said in the impulse of the moment, because it was in my heart, hardly thinking whom I addressed. Had I known, I might have hesitated, for fear of giving offence: for here, as at New Orleans, I was among Confederates. Before me sat General Basil Duke, the brother-in-law of the noted chief, John Morgan, with whom he made the famous raid into Ohio, where he was captured and imprisoned at Columbus six months! Such a man might not relish allusions to the past, yet I had hardly sat down before he rushed up to me with open arms, and seemed ready to embrace me. If he had done so, I should have returned it with a heartiness that would have satisfied the most warm-blooded Kentuckian. Others came up, saying, "I want to take your hand," and "If men like you would come down South, they would do a world of good." I hope my readers will not think me so foolish as to repeat these words because of the compliment to myself. I repeat them only to show the temper of the South: that the old bitterness is wearing away, and that Southern men are quick to respond to patriotic sentiments. Of course, if a Northern man goes South and is rude and offensive, he will meet, as he deserves, sharp rebuffs. But a little tact and common sense, combined with genuine good feeling, will go far to remove irritation, and smooth the way, not only to "reconciliation," but to a warmer love to each

other than ever before, and to the great country to which
they as well as we belong.

But enough of personalities. The carriages are at the
door, and for the next two or three hours we are driving
about the city. How beautiful it is, with its wide streets
and long avenues, lined with handsome residences! They
have not yet learned the New York style of architecture
which piles story upon story, mounting up to sky-parlors,
which can only be reached by elevators! Why should they,
so long as they have room to spread out nearer the warm
breast of mother earth? Almost universally the better
houses stand apart, each in its plot of ground, with light
and air on every side; while in many cases the open lawns
bloom with flowers, and doors and windows are wreathed
with clustering vines. What magnificence of architecture
can equal this natural beauty? In riding about Louisville,
I felt the same sort of pleasure as in our most beautiful
New England cities, such, for example, as New Haven and
Hartford, and Springfield, Mass. These homes, so beautiful without and so happy within, are a nation's security.
We may have strikes in cities, with scenes of confusion and
disorder; but that nation is safe which is " fast-anchored "
by millions of happy homes.

Of public institutions, Louisville has its full share. It
was my good fortune to be in the carriage with an excellent
Presbyterian elder, who pointed out to me the fine school
buildings, with hospitals and asylums, which show that
the work of charity is not forgotten by the warm Southern
heart.

If we say this of the city, what shall we say of the State
and the people? Kentucky is the daughter of Virginia,
and a proud mother makes a proud daughter. Meet Kentuckians where you will, at home or abroad, you find them
proud of their State. They are eloquent of its natural
beauty and fertility, and—if they do not all go to the ex-

tent of the negro preacher, who could find no description of heaven so satisfactory to his imagination as that " it was a Kentucky kind of a place," yet—should there be found any word of Scripture to warrant a Biblical argument, I verily believe that their theologians would enter the field to prove that the original Paradise created for man was in the Blue Grass Region of Kentucky! That region is indeed a Paradise now—a Paradise " after the fall." The eastern portion of the State, which borders on the Ohio, and of which Lexington is the center, is a land as beautiful as can be found beneath the sun. The soil is of great fertility, and the earth yields her increase in abundance for the wants of man. The possessors have grown rich, as they show, not only by their broad acres and fat cattle and blooded horses, but by their stately mansions, surrounded by wide lawns and shaded by magnificent trees.

As we come closer to a people, and get a nearer view of them by seeing their home-life, it may help us in our present study to introduce a quiet domestic scene.

Some years ago a picture was exhibited in New York, painted by my dear friend, Eastman Johnson, who is so justly famous for his " interiors," entitled " The Old Kentucky Home." But it was only part of a home, and the poorest part, though not perhaps the least joyous. In the rear of an old mansion were the negro quarters, against which rested a " lean-to" which showed signs of the ravages of time. The roof had fallen in, and the side had fallen out; but this uncovered side disclosed a fire-place that suggested the " hoe-cake baking," which once made that old kitchen a scene of daily festivity, and caused the black faces to shine as they gleamed in the fire-light. In front of this " chimney-piece" was a group which might well have made a study for a painter. An old darkey, leaning back in his seat, was playing on a banjo, while the mistress of his affections was seated at his feet, and the pickaninnies were scattered around. A negro mother, with her baby in her arms, leaned out of an upper window to catch the entrancing melody, or perhaps to keep watch of a young man and maiden who were making love in a corner. The only white faces that appeared were those of two ladies of the family, who peeped out of a garden door, and smiled with delight at the scene. It was a picture of the old plantation days, when these careless, happy creatures, at the first touch of the banjo, would go off into spasms of delight, would sing a song or dance a jig, while masters and mistresses looked on indulgently at the irrepressible gayety of the simple African race. It was a pretty way to suggest the relation of kindliness and sympathy which united the two classes together: "the high" made happy by seeing the happiness of "the humble."

This gives us a picture of master and servant which is not according to our usual idea of slavery, but which had its counterpart in thousands of Southern homes. The wrong of slavery was in the *power* which it gave to the owner, and which, if he were a hard master, permitted him to carry it to the extreme of cruelty. But it would be a mistake to suppose that this power was always abused. On the contrary, masters and mistresses often felt a great affection and tenderness for those of the subject race with whom they had been brought up from childhood, and whose fate was so closely bound up with their own; and cases were not wanting in which they tried to protect these helpless creatures, even when they were themselves overwhelmed with disaster. One of this kind has recently come to my knowledge.

More than half a century ago there lived in Kentucky a lady in whom were united several honored names—those of her father and grandfather, both distinguished in the early history of the State, and that of her husband, a brother of John J. Crittenden, who was second in popular favor only to Henry Clay. Her husband died in the prime of manhood, leaving his young widow with an insolvent estate and five children. Compelled thus early in life to face a hard future, her anxiety, next to that for her own children, was for her servants, who were liable to be seized by the sheriff and sold, to be taken South to the plantations of the Lower Mississippi. In such a crisis this brave woman stood between them and the law as their protector. She asked only that she might be allowed the management of a factory belonging to the estate, called a " rope-walk," that made a coarse cloth for the baling of cotton, which was conceded to her, and which she conducted with such diligence and prudence, like the woman in the Proverbs, " rising early in the morning and putting her hands to the distaff," that in three years she had earned enough to redeem her servants from the fate that was impending over them. " And," said my informant, " forty years after I saw those very negroes, then gray-headed men, lift up tenderly the coffin that contained the body of their old mistress (to whom, as they were free, they were bound by no allegiance but that of love and gratitude), and with streaming eyes carry her to her grave."

This touching story tempts me to go a step further, and to say that this noble woman was the mother of a race of brave men, one of whom lately ruled that most turbulent element in our country, the Mormons of Utah, in which trying and difficult position he showed a firmness and courage worthy of such a mother. In a late New York paper I find the following notice of mother and son:

" The mother of ex-Gov. Murray of Utah was a remarkable woman. Her first husband was the brother of the noble and eloquent John J. Crittenden, and one of her sons was the recent Governor of Missouri. When I first saw Mrs. Murray, it was in her own beautiful Kentucky home on the Ohio river. I think I never saw a more magnificent-

looking couple than Col. and Mrs. Murray. The latter was
tall and stately, almost statuesque in her beauty. She was
a veritable *grande dame*, but her dignity was tempered
with the sweetest gentleness. She was, moreover, a woman of great intellect and character. Another son by her
first marriage was a brilliant young fellow, brave and
dashing as a knight of old, who sacrificed himself years ago
on a filibustering expedition to Cuba, that maelstrom that
swallowed up so many bright and unselfish, but misguided
souls of the Southern chivalry. Young Crittenden, in
company with other leaders of the expedition, was captured
and sentenced to death. One by one, at sunrise, his comrades stood before a line of Cuban rifles, and at the order
knelt, and received a volley in their ill-fated breasts.
When Crittenden's turn came, he refused to kneel, saying:
'A Kentuckian kneels to none but his God,' and despite
threats, oaths, and orders, he received the fatal shots erect
and motionless. Years ago the favorite song in drawing-
rooms throughout Kentucky and the South was a pathetic
ballad founded on these last words, and bearing on the
title-page a picture of this dauntless young spirit. Mrs.
Murray was revered and honored by all who knew her."

The sons of such a mother could not but be brave. They
have shown their courage in most difficult circumstances.
Gov. Crittenden of Missouri had a peculiar work to perform. The western part of that State was infested with
gangs of robbers, who, secreting themselves in the darkest
and loneliest places of the forest, lay in wait for railway
trains, which they brought to a halt by obstructions on the
track, and then shot the engineers, and "went through"
the passengers in the most approved style of highwaymen.
Such was the terror inspired by these frequent raids, that
many travellers avoided the State. And yet it was a most
difficult task to seize, convict, and punish the robbers.
How difficult we may judge by remembering how many

years it took the Italian Government to put down brigand-
age in Calabria and Sicily. The attempt was connected
with great personal dangers. The Governor was in constant receipt of threats of assassination. But he never
hesitated a moment, and executed his trust so effectively
that to-day Missouri has peace and quietness in all her borders.

A still more difficult task was that in Utah, as the Mormons were numbered by tens of thousands. But Gov.
Murray had had a training in war. He was a gallant officer
in the Union army, and after Kilpatrick was wounded had
command of the cavalry in Sherman's March to the Sea.
When he went to Utah, people found that they had no
child to deal with, no weak Governor who could be either
frightened or fooled. While he did them no injustice, he
held the reins with a firm hand. They gnashed their teeth
at him, but at the same time " walked softly " before him.
The best testimony to the wisdom and vigor of his administration, was the universal regret of the Gentiles at his
retirement. Such sons are living witnesses to the great
qualities of her whose blood flows in their veins—one who
was more than a Roman matron, an American mother.

XIII.

SOME of my friends who profess to enjoy reading what I write still have a quiet smile now and then at my enthusiasms. They tell me that I find good in every country and in every people; that, as I see beauty in the sands of the desert, so I find something to admire and to love in the most unattractive specimens of humanity. For example, they say: " Why do you go crazy about those Kentuckians? Don't you know that they are a pugnacious and combative race, given to hatreds and revenges, and always fighting with somebody? If they have no outside enemies to fight, they fight with one another. They fly in a passion for the most trifling cause, and then out comes a horsewhip or a pistol or a bowie-knife! You can not take up a newspaper without seeing a story of a street-fight in a town in Kentucky. Somebody has had ' a difficulty ' with somebody else, and one or the other has been shot down in cold blood. Nor are these affrays confined to individuals; they pass from a man to his family; brothers and sons take up the quarrel, till a whole circle of kindred is involved, and not unfrequently it becomes an hereditary feud, that passes down from generation to generation. A strange people indeed to be held up as the highest type of American chivalry!"

Of the atrocity of these things, it is impossible to speak

in too severe condemnation. I make no apology for them, for apology there is none. They are deeds that belong only to savages, and not to civilized men. But they are not every-day occurrences; nor are they common to the whole population. If inquired into, they will be found to be most frequent among gamblers and sporting men, by whom it would be very unjust to judge a whole State. While these ornaments of society amuse themselves now and then by shooting each other, the mass of the people go about their business, leading quiet and peaceable lives in all godliness and honesty.

The feuds between families, which we are accustomed to impute to Kentucky, as a stain upon her fair name, should rather be imputed to the whole South. A clergyman who was born in Kentucky, but who has passed the greater part of his life still further South, tells me that he has known similar feuds in Mississippi and in Louisiana—on the Red River, and in the beautiful Téche country. But that does not make them any better. The "Vendetta," which in Sicily and Corsica is looked upon as a relic of pure savagery, surviving in the midst of European civilization, is not changed in character when transferred to American soil.

But however much of this spirit may be due to natural temperament, it has been intensified by several causes. I am sorry to say that Kentucky is the great whiskey-producing State in the Union. When I strolled out of the Galt House to take my first walk in Louisville, it seemed to me, by the number of warehouses devoted to the storage of whiskey, that it must be the principal product of Kentucky. The famous "Bourbon Whiskey" takes its name from Bourbon county, which lies in the very heart of the Blue Grass region. With such a river of fire running through the State, what can be expected of a people whose hot blood only needs this added stimulant to be inflamed beyond control?

But he who would trace the genesis of the fighting temper of Kentucky and of the South, must bring into the foreground another potent cause. This quick resentment and this habit of violence, showing itself in fights and feuds, Corsican Vendetta and all, is the heir-loom of Slavery—one of the natural products of irresponsible power. Whoever has given into his hand absolute mastery over other human beings, must needs have extraordinary self-control not to become a tyrant on a small scale, or a large scale, as the case may be. He who from a boy has been approached with servility by inferiors, does not bear contradiction with composure even from equals. A slight irritation will send the blood to his heart, and the quick answer to his lips. Added to this in the old days was the temptation of an idle life. When all menial labor was performed by slaves, the young "men of family" had little to do but to keep up the reputation of gentlemen; and this was gained in no way so readily as by the exhibition of courage. One must be tenacious of points of honor, and be prepared to resent all real or imagined injuries. Not unfrequently a young "blood" picked a quarrel, that he might show his courage in fighting a duel. To have fought and "killed his man" gave him a certain reputation. But these things are far less frequent than they once were. A duel is now a rare occurrence. A relic of barbarism, it is passing away with the advance of civilization. And so of other forms of violence, which were the natural outgrowth of Slavery: now that Slavery is gone, they can not long survive. As Slavery was the brood-mother of many forms of cruelty, now that the old witch-hag that gave them birth is dead, it is fit that her ill-shapen offspring should die and be buried in the same dishonored grave.

But with all my attempts to explain, if not to explain *away*, the belligerent temper of the Kentuckians, I am afraid I shall have to admit that it is partly in the blood.

There is no denying that they are a people of ardent temperament, in which they resemble the Southern peoples of Europe, the Spaniards and Italians, rather than the colder races of the North. Such a people will sometimes enter into combat for the mere pleasure of the excitement—the *gaudium certaminis*—the opportunity it gives for the exercise of courage and of strength; and will even welcome a conflict that calls them to measure their powers with a worthy foe.

If we are disposed to condemn this severely, we should remember that the same fiery temper has sometimes divided the Church, and alienated Christian men. Religion does not change wholly a man's nature; it only sets it working in a new direction. I will not say that the average Kentuckian is of such a high-strung spirit that it takes more grace to convert him than other men; but even Divine grace conforms to the peculiar nature of the individual. Though he be converted, and become a Christian, he is a Kentucky Christian, and his spirit is sometimes so hot within him that it must overflow. If it can not show itself on the field of battle or the field of honor, it will find vent in politics, at the polls or in the courts, or even in the churches.

Nay, ministers of the Gospel sometimes show themselves unrelenting and unforgiving. Not long since the grave closed over two men who had no superiors in the Church; both sound in the faith—no hickory-tree in all the forests of Kentucky was sounder; both learned and eloquent; yet who somehow could not "consort" together, and whose peculiar regard for each other is one of the traditions of the State. We refer to this, not to magnify an unhappy difference, but to show how the grace of God may live (*and burn*) in such warrior-breasts. But time is the gentle healer of all wounds, or at least it covers them with oblivion. Robert Breckinridge and Stuart Robinson have gone to the grave; the grass grows green over the places where they sleep; and as we think of them now, it is not of the causes which divided them, but that in this at least they were one —as lion-hearted champions for the faith of the Gospel.

A people may sometimes be wiser than their teachers, taking heed to avoid their errors, as well as to imitate their virtues. But even though Kentuckians may put away all hatred and malice, they will not sink down into being tame and spiritless. They never were, and never will be, a meek and lamb-like race. Indeed I should be sorry to think that they could ever lose their ancient spirit, though they may exercise it in new fields—fields more worthy of their ambition. They will always be, more or less, a fighting people; and to this the sternest moralists must be a little indulgent. It will never do in this latitude to count a mild degree of combativeness an unpardonable sin, for " who then can be saved?" All that the wisest can do is to guide what they can not wholly repress. If they have to deal with a people who are excitable, and ready to start at the tap of the drum, they must be content to turn their heads the right way; so that if they must fight, they will fight on the right side.

If in this picture I have seemed to make the colors rather dark, such a background will only set in brighter relief the lights that are thrown upon it. The faults of the Kentuckian, be they great or small, are of the open kind, that do not shun the light of day, instead of the mean and low that hide in darkness. His virtues and his vices, wide apart as they are, are yet fed by the same abounding life that is in him. The spirit that makes him quick to resent a wrong, makes him equally quick to recognize a kindness. Thus the good and the bad alike are far more demonstrative because of his warm, impulsive nature. He is a hot-blooded creature, and whatever he does, he does with all the intensity of his being: he loves and he hates; he is a warm friend and a bitter enemy. Such a man we can love, not in spite of his faults, but we might almost say because of them, as they are the manifestations of a frank, manly, and generous spirit. It is easier to form attachments to a people who have warm blood, even if they do quarrel with us once in a while, than to make friends with those who are cold as icebergs, whose sluggish blood creeps slowly through their veins. Among such a people will be found men and women after the pattern of the family to which I have referred. A race, capable of producing such specimens of manhood and womanhood, is not a common race. The people have a character of their own, which is as marked as the geography of the State. Their very physique is a striking one. It is often observed that they are above the average height; that they are tall, well formed, and of commanding presence. This uncommon stature has been ascribed to the fact that Kentucky is a limestone country. It is said that the lime in "the springs which run among the hills," passes into the blood of men, and makes their bones of iron. In support of this theory, it is said that to the same cause in the soil is owing the marvellous fertility of the Blue Grass region, which produces other species of animated nature of the same superior quality; that it "grows" splendid horses and cattle, as well as men of uncommon vigor. Whatever be the cause, the fact is apparent to every observer that the Kentuckians are a stalwart race.

From this physique it comes in part that they are a race of brave men—in part, I say, for courage is not wholly a physical trait, but results from a combination of the physical with the moral, bodily strength being united with force of character. It is no great merit for a Kentuckian to be brave, for we can not think of him as anything else. Courage is with him a tradition and an inheritance. His fathers were brave before him, from the time when

Daniel Boone crossed the mountains with his rifle on his shoulder. From a boy he is trained to ride a horse and to handle a gun, and hence he takes naturally to military pursuits, into which he enters with his accustomed ardor. In the late war Kentuckians fought on both sides; yet wherever they fought, they fought bravely. The position of the State was one of extreme difficulty. Lying on the border between the North and the South, she was opposed to disunion, and wholly disapproved of the action of the hotheads of South Carolina. But when the crisis came, many of those who were unfavorable to secession, still could not take up arms against their brethren. A chivalrous feeling led them to take part with the weaker side; and so the people divided—some going one way, and some another. The line was drawn through cities and villages, severing communities and churches, and even families, literally setting brother against brother. In this violence of feeling, the State was not only drawn apart, but we might almost say, was "drawn and quartered." But the bravest fighters are often the quickest to be reconciled when the contest is over. Those who have been foremost in the day of battle are most prompt to recognize the fate of war, and to lay down their hatreds when they lay down their arms. To-day this State is as loyal as Massachusetts, and if a foreign war were to come, I believe the country would have no braver defenders than the Confederate soldiers of Kentucky.

It is not necessary to enlarge the catalogue of virtues. It is enough to say that the Kentuckian is a man built on a large pattern, with a frame made alike for action and for endurance. He stands erect, and carries himself with a manly air in his open face and direct look, as of one who has his place in the world—a place of which he need not be ashamed. His moral qualities partake of his physical: as he is broad-breasted, so he is large-hearted—open, frank, generous; a man to be respected, and to be feared by anybody who would wrong him; but whose cordial manners and abounding hospitality win the heart of the stranger within his gates. He has his faults, but who would remember faults which are redeemed by such splendid virtues? Nor is this high praise to be given to men only, for if they are distinguished for courage, no less are their sisters for beauty and goodness; so that to Kentucky may be applied the proud boast on the monument of a noble house in Westminster Abbey, that " all her sons are brave, and all her daughters virtuous."

Such were the thoughts that lingered within me as we left Louisville at evening, and fled away in the stillness of the night. Sitting at the window, and looking out at the villages through which we passed, and watching the lights that twinkled by hundreds of firesides (as on the night that we began our journey) the same pictures rose to the fancy of the scenes within: of the groups around the family table, where fathers and mothers looked proudly into the faces of their happy children! With such a vision fading on the sight, my heart went out in one last word, God bless the Old Kentucky Home!

And now, as we are about to cross the border, I turn a lingering look to the beautiful South-land where we have received so much kindness, and invoke upon her the Oriental benediction of " Peace!"—the one word which comprises all earthly good. Never again can we feel that we are strangers here. Kindred in blood, we are brothers in heart; and to the South, as fervently as to the North, do I say: Peace be within your walls and prosperity within your palaces! Peace on your mountains and your valleys, and in all your happy homes! Good-night!

FIVE VOLUMES OF TRAVEL.

BY REV. HENRY M. FIELD, D.D.

Published by Charles Scribner's Sons, New York.

ROUND THE WORLD.

In Two Volumes (Fifteenth Edition).

" **Two as interesting and valuable Books of Travel as have been published in this Country.**"—NEW YORK EXPRESS.

I.—FROM THE LAKES OF KILLARNEY TO THE GOLDEN HORN.

One volume, Crown 8vo. Price, $2.00.

From the London Times.

"As we all know, it is not necessary for a man to discover a new country in order to write an interesting book of travel. He may traverse the most beaten track in Europe, and yet if he can describe what he has seen with freshness and originality, he will succeed in engaging our attention. We do not go far with Dr. Field before finding out that he is a traveller of this sort." And so on for a column and a half, criticising here and there, but praising warmly; and ending, "Thus we take leave of a writer who has produced so interesting and meritorious a book that we are sorry we cannot coincide with all his conclusions."

From the New York Tribune.

"Few recent travellers combine so many qualities that are adapted to command the interest and sympathy of the public. While he indulges, to its fullest extent, the characteristic American curiosity with regard to foreign lands, insisting on seeing every object of interest with his own eyes, shrinking from no peril or difficulty in pursuit of information—climbing mountains, descending mines, exploring pyramids, with no sense of satiety or weariness—he has also made a faithful study of the highest authorities on the different subjects of his narrative, thus giving solidity and depth to his descriptions, without sacrificing their facility or grace."

From the late William Adams, D.D., LL.D.

" . . . They are the best [Sketches of Travel] of the kind ever written, and have done, and will do, the writer boundless credit."

ROUND THE WORLD,

Volume II.—*FROM EGYPT TO JAPAN.* (Price $2.00.)

From R. D. Hitchcock, D.D., LL.D., President of the Union Theological Seminary, New York.

"In this second volume, Dr. Field, I think, has surpassed himself in the first, and this is saying a good deal. In both volumes the editorial instinct and habit are conspicuous. Dr. Prime has said that an editor should have six senses, the sixth being a 'sense of the *interesting*.' Dr. Field has this to perfection."

From the New York Observer.

"The present volume comprises by far the most novel, romantic, and interesting part of the Journey [Round the World], and the story of it is told and the scenes are painted by the hand of a master."

From the New York Herald.

"It would be impossible by extracts to convey an adequate idea of the abundance or picturesque freshness of these sketches of travel, without copying a large part of the book."

From Rev. R. S. Storrs, D.D., LL.D.

"It is indeed a charming book—full of fresh information, picturesque description, and thoughtful studies of men, countries, and civilizations."

From Rev. Dr. A. P. Peabody, late Editor of the North American Review.

"I have never, within anything like the same space, seen so much said of Egypt, or so wisely or so well. Much as I have read about Egypt—many volumes indeed—I have found some of these descriptions more graphic, more realistic, than I have ever met, or expect to meet, elsewhere."

By Charles Dudley Warner, in the Hartford Courant.

"It is thoroughly entertaining; the reader's interest is never allowed to flag. The author carries us forward from land to land with uncommon vivacity, enlivens the way with a good humor, a careful observation, and treats all people with a refreshing liberality."

From the Newark Advertiser.

"'FROM THE LAKES OF KILLARNEY TO THE GOLDEN HORN,' and 'FROM EGYPT TO JAPAN,' are justly considered as among the best modern books of travel."

ON THE DESERT.

1 vol., Crown 8vo. Price, $2.00.

An Account of a Journey in the track of the Israelites along the Red Sea, among the Peaks of Sinai, through the Desert of the Wandering, and up to the Promised Land.

From Rev. C. H. Spurgeon, of London.

"Wonderful! Subject, the Desert; discourse, a book of the first order. . . . It would be difficult to meet with a more lively and instructive work. Surely the monks of Sinai, the Bedaween and their camels, and all the other appurtenances of the Great and Terrible Wilderness, are now done—done to a turn, done to the very utmost. Our traveller used all his eyes, and he seems to have possessed hidden optics in the back of his head and the heels of his boots. He gathers more from the Desert than most men would have gleaned in the Gardens of Solomon. This admirable work will enjoy a wide popularity, and become a standard book of reference."

From Archdeacon Farrar, Westminster Abbey.

"I found it so interesting, that I could not lay it down till I had finished it."

From Noah Swayne, LL.D., late Justice of the Supreme Court of the United States.

"Although I had been over the same ground before with Dean Stanley and others, I find the work extremely interesting."

From Prof. W. G. T. Shedd, D.D.

"I see the Desert and the mountains, and the Arabs, and the camels, and all the strange scenery, without the toil, heat, and danger."

From Rev. T. W. Chambers, D.D., of New York, who made the Journey across the Desert to Mount Sinai in 1874.

"The reader will get a better idea of the real characteristics of the Sinaitic Desert and its inhabitants from these pages, than from any other accessible volume. Those who have been over the ground will bear witness to the author's literal accuracy."

From the New York Herald.

"There is not an uninteresting chapter in the book. It is entertaining throughout. It depicts men and countries in a picturesque and thoughtful manner, and is likely to meet with as much favor as the author's former capital books of travel."

THE GREEK ISLANDS
AND TURKEY AFTER THE WAR.

1 vol., 12mo, with Maps and Illustrations, $1.50.

From Rev. Dr. Washburn, President of Robert College, Constantinople.

"I have read it with the greatest interest, and with constant admiration of the accuracy of its statements."

From the Morning Journal (New York).

"More fascinating than nine-tenths of the novels published during the past year, is Dr. Henry M. Field's 'THE GREEK ISLANDS AND TURKEY AFTER THE WAR.' It is a modern Childe Harold Pilgrimage, purified and ennobled—a panorama of lovely scenes, rendered sacred by apostolic memories, and ever interesting through historical and poetical associations.

From the Critic (New York).

"We know of no writer on travel over beaten paths who excels Dr. Field. We do not place him second to Miss Bird or De Amicis. These in their way may be more brilliant, higher-colored, piquant; but they are less trustworthy, and have not

'The years that bring the philosophic mind.'

Our American editor-author is more sunny, meditative, accurate, sympathetic, and knows at a glance what is interesting. He is never tedious. While the vessel of his thought brims with quotable felicities of expression, and is beaded with wit and fancy, it is rich with the vintage of philosophic culture. After an ordinary lifetime spent in studying men and events, and training his pen to make pictures and write histories in paragraphs, this son of America sallies forth from his sanctum. He first steams round the globe, and shakes out of his quill a pair of literary twins that have entered their—we know not what thousandth. Then perhaps with a mild twinge of shame at going so fast, he rambles "ON THE DESERT" and "AMONG THE HOLY HILLS"; and now, just when we want it, he seems but to touch an electric button, and *presto !* the timely book is on our table.

"If there were any best among his five volumes, which are all excellent, we should aver that it is this, the author's last."

AMONG THE HOLY HILLS.

1 vol., 12mo, with a Map, $1.50.